A MANHATTAN MURDER MYSTERY

AN IRINA CURTIUS MYSTERY

SUSAN BERNHARDT

Northwoods Books
Cover Art Copyright 2016 by SKB Arts
First eBook Edition 2016
First Print Edition 2018

ISBN: 978-1-98326-963-9

PRAISE FOR SUSAN BERNHARDT AND
A MANHATTAN MURDER MYSTERY

"While reading this book, I felt like I was watching a classic murder mystery movie. It reminded me of the Alfred Hitchcock movies. All of the plot lines are expertly woven together and so detailed that it is hard to catch your breath when reading this story." ~Mary Brown, MJB Reviewers

"Susan deftly weaves her suspenseful story within the confines of the Brownstone, giving the reader a deliciously voyeuristic peek into the lives of its tenants."
~Margaret Mendel, Kings River Life Magazine

"A Manhattan Murder Mystery" is like a love letter to this great city and it's obvious that the author respects New Yorkers and how we live here." ~Sharon Katz, Sleuth Cafe

"An intricately crafted plot makes this mystery intriguing!!"
~Jean Baldikoski, Literary critic

"I love the cozy feel of the worlds Susan Bernhardt creates. She welcomes you into the story with a refined finesse only a talented writer can conjure, and doesn't let you leave until all the pieces of the mystery fit together."
~Jo-Ann Carson, author

"Once again Susan Bernhardt shares her great storytelling skills with readers. She carefully draws characters and describes settings so a reader feels like she is a part of the scene." ~J.Q. Rose, author

For my loving and supportive husband,
my two wonderful sons and their lovely wives,
and my adorable grandson.
—With love —

Acknowledgements

I am delighted to acknowledge and thank my friend, Lorenzo Martinez, for reading my chapters and providing me with insightful suggestions. Thank you to my dear husband, Bill Bernhardt, who listened to my chapters and made wonderful observations and suggestions. I'd like to thank my talented son, Peter Bernhardt, who I consulted with for ideas for parts of this mystery. I would also like to thank my stellar line editor, Linda Roden, for her fabulous work. Thank you to the talented Kenneth Hicks, who provided the photograph for the book cover. I'd also like to thank Anne Rusert for my photograph on the back cover.

I am blessed with an incredible support system; my family and friends and my readers. Thank you for your ongoing support and for spreading the word of my mysteries.

A MANHATTAN
MURDER MYSTERY

Chapter One

Friday, February 13

The last notes of Für Elise were still resonating as the children finished their ballet exercise routine.

I clapped. "That was lovely children. All right, everyone have a wonderful Valentine's weekend. I have a valentine to give each of you before you leave."

Ivy, a little girl with hair in French braids came up to me and touched my arm.

"Well, Ivy, how did you like your first ballet class?"

Her eyes sparkled. "Very much so, Miss Irina. But when do we get to dance?" She gave me an expectant look.

I smiled. "Ivy, as I mentioned, learning to dance is about exercises and stretching our bodies. You may have to work even harder to catch up with the other children. But you'll be dancing before too long. You'll see."

After all of the children were picked up, I said to Jerome who was packing up his things, "That was a great choice at the end."

He smiled, his mouth wide with large expressive lips. "Can't go wrong with Beethoven." He ran his fingers through his brown, shaggy hair.

I nodded. Jerome was a friend from my college days, whom I met in a coffeehouse where he was a regular. His improvisations on the baby grand piano made the crowds go silent. Semi-retired, he volunteered his time, a few hours each week, to play for my classes. His other non-paying gig was in the summer, where I listened to him play numerous times in Washington Square Park, his outdoor theatre.

Jerome smiled shyly as he put the last of his music into his bag. "Do you have plans tomorrow evening for Valentine's? I thought you might want to go out for a bite to eat."

"Thanks. That's kind of you, but I've already made plans with Margarite for dinner." Margarite was my best friend who lived in the apartment down the hall from mine.

He put on his black wool coat over his old green sweater that had seen better days and buttoned up. "After dinner, you and she could meet me at The Vanguard for a drink." His voice took a more insistent tone.

I shrugged my shoulders. Perhaps he was lonely. "I'll see how we feel."

He pursed his lips. "Margarite will be fine with it."

Way past insistent. Almost demanding. This wasn't like the easy going Jerome I knew, who seldom took himself or anything seriously. I raised an eyebrow and picked up a towel someone had left on the floor and placed it in the hamper. What was this all about?

Jerome started for the door. "See you tomorrow evening then. Let's say about nine-thirty."

Not having a chance to respond, I watched as he walked outside past the large window of the studio. While musing over our conversation, I noticed a young man walk by that I had seen on several occasions lately. Quite handsome in a rugged way, he had reddish-brown curly hair and looked familiar. Did I know him from somewhere? Was he new to the neighborhood? He glanced into the studio. I smiled. He looked ahead and kept walking. Probably didn't even see me.

When changing into my street clothes in the back room, I looked in the mirror. I no longer had that lean and lithe look of a ballet dancer. My waist was starting to widen, but I still had the long slender neck and strong legs. I did a petit jêté and smiled. I gathered my things and locked up.

It was freezing out. There was a late wintry mix of snow and sleet. Tiny hail started to fall. I pulled my scarf higher up around my neck. Everyone was hurrying, trying to get indoors as soon as possible. I hustled a few blocks through the slushy mess to Back to Eden Bakery.

Opening the door, the bell above it tinkled. I was immediately welcomed with the ethereal smells and warmth that emanated from within. Back to Eden Bakery was my little slice of heaven on the Upper West Side of Manhattan. I eyed their well-stocked case, then chose a table by the window in the narrow café. When my favorite waiter came over, I ordered a cup of chia tea and an almond fruit tart. As I stared out the window, watching the pedestrian activity on the street and the taxis and town cars weaving in and out, I thought about how much I loved this neighborhood. Its energy infected me.

I had a love affair with New York City and lived on the Upper West Side most of my life. It had a down-to-earth, authentic feel and a sense of community in a global culture. Unlike what most people thought, I found the people friendly; everyone seemed to have a story that they'd love to share and in turn, they were interested in hearing yours. The city had an eclectic mix of art, music, performing art, and great restaurants, new and old that had any food imaginable.

My order arrived. I took a sip of the tea, a perfect blend of spice. I added a couple of spoonfuls of sugar, then looked out the window again. And my work was here. I loved teaching ballet to young children, children like Ivy, with her dreams of one day becoming a ballerina. Children like her who visited the Met and looked up at Degas' sculpture of the "Little Dancer" with stars in their eyes. Dreams of futures.

The door opened and with it a cold blast of air. Another customer. At least it had stopped hailing and the sun was out. I took a taste of the fluted-edged pastry crust. It was sweet and the cream and fruit, luscious. I put the fork back down on the plate. Tomorrow was Valentine's Day. Visions arose of a Valentine's date decades ago, when an ex-boyfriend and I went skating at Wollman Rink in Central Park. Afterwards, back in our cozy apartment, we made fondue and laughed as we fed each other chocolate covered strawberries. I could still hear the smooth sound of jazz in the background and feel the warmth of ... Stop! Stop!

I shook my head and finished my tea. Why did I still think of those and the other Valentines I wanted to forget? That was so long ago, in another lifetime. Forty years should have been long enough to sear the wounds. I was happy to be having Valentine's dinner with Margarite, tomorrow evening. And now of course, followed by the obligatory drink with Jerome afterwards.

Bundled back up, I stopped off at a Korean market on the way home, looked over the flowers, and chose a gorgeous bouquet of white lilies and pink roses with a variety of greens. I always thought of flowers as nature's artwork. After standing in line for a good ten minutes, I made sure the bouquet was double wrapped in plastic, and went on my way.

I lived on the first floor of an ivy-covered brownstone built in the late 19th century on West 87th Street between Columbus and Amsterdam. There were three units on my floor. Holding on to the ornate cement handrails of my building, I climbed the icy stairs, that the late afternoon sun would hopefully melt, and opened the heavy glass door, where I saw my neighbor, Stephen Kramer, slamming the door to his apartment.

I walked into the entrance hall. "Hello Stephen. How—"

He looked up, his eyes protruding. Dark circles surrounded his eyes and his skin had a grayish tinge. Just this past summer I had commented to his wife, Tricia, how they both looked the picture of health after they had returned from a bike outing. I abruptly turned to the side and backed up close to the mahogany staircase which led to the second floor, so he wouldn't collide with me in his haste.

He mumbled something incoherent as he passed by in a hurry. After he stormed out the front door, I went over and knocked on their door. He and Tricia must have been fighting again. I removed the plastic from the flowers as I waited so they wouldn't be crushed, then glanced at my watch. Four o'clock. Tricia opened the door with her coat on. "Tricia, are you going out?"

"No, I just came home. I got off of work early, but it still felt like a long day."

I wouldn't talk long. "I noticed Stephen leaving in a huff. What's up with him? So completely out of character...he looks like death warmed over. He should see—"

She clicked her tongue. Tricia was a warm person, yet cool. "Really, Irina, he doesn't look that bad."

Oh, yes, he did.

She started to unbutton her coat. "He's overworked and puts in a lot of overtime. He has a lot of stress at work."

And at home.

"But still has time to play racquetball with Alex," I heard Alice call out from inside the apartment. Alice was Tricia's sister.

"You'd think racquetball would help relieve stress," I said.

Tricia shrugged. "Stephen's often like this after an evening with his friend, Alex. Irina, what lovely flowers."

I looked at the bouquet I was holding. Why not. "Here...they're for you." After I saw the state Stephen was in, even if Tricia denied it, I thought she could use a pick-me-up.

"How sweet. Thank you. Would you like to come in?"

I entered their living room. Even with the low winter sun, we had great afternoon light in the brownstone. She took her coat off and hung it up in the front closet near the door. She reached for my coat and hung mine up as well. "I was going to make a pot of tea. Would you like to join us?"

Her upper arms had bruises. Had she been grabbed roughly? I had seen bruising like this often and had just worked yesterday at SAFE Inc., a women and children's shelter where I volunteered.

"Thank you. That sounds lovely." It looked like an intervention might be needed.

I followed Tricia into her tiny kitchen. She was a striking woman, blonde, long-limbed, and beautiful without makeup, although today she wore plenty, outlining her large emerald-green eyes. She had a small upturned nose and high cheek bones. Her straight, shoulder-length hair was pulled back for a casual look. She had previously mentioned she dabbled in modeling after college.

Tricia filled the teapot with water and put it on the stove. She then proceeded to cut the bottom of the stems off the flowers and arrange them into a crystal vase she had taken out of the cupboard. "These flowers are beautiful."

"Hana Asian Market has the best flowers around," I said.

"That's where we usually get ours from as well."

I glanced around. Compared to the rest of her modern apartment, her kitchen was a bit dated and messy. Bowls of herbs covered much of the counters. Dirty dishes lay in the sink. She closed the dishwasher that had been opened. It looked full. Before Alice had moved in, the kitchen was always tidy. Tricia and Stephen, both working during the day, usually ate most of their dinners out.

"Sorry about the mess. We were cooking yesterday and didn't get a chance to clean up yet."

"Tricia, what happened to your arms?"

She reached for a pale blush sweater that was on the back of a kitchen chair and put it on. "Oh, it's nothing."

I didn't really believe Stephen had it in him, but thought I should ask, "Stephen?"

14

She didn't respond. She added tea leaves to the pot and some herbs that looked like mint from a plate next to her herb mill. She and her sister were herb fanatics. She went back to her flower arranging.

I had often heard Tricia and Stephen arguing in the hallway or in their apartment when one or the other was leaving. It was often about Alice. "You shouldn't have to put up with this," I continued. "You can call the police."

"The police?" She said in a somewhat shrill voice. "I said it's nothing." She looked up at me. Her voice returned to normal. "Really."

Alice came into the room giving me a dagger, side-eye glance with her brown eyes, her demeanor cold and confident. She had moved into the two-bedroom home with Tricia and Stephen this past September. More serious and quiet of the two sisters, I often found her in a sullen mood. "What are you talking about, the police?"

"I was about to tell Irina, I knocked my arms while moving paintings at work today."

In her silence when I asked, she led me to believe it could have been Stephen. I was relieved to know that wasn't the case.

Tricia turned to me looking more relaxed. "By the way, did you know the Impressionist Fashion in Art exhibition started today?" Tricia worked part time in one of the curatorial departments at The Metropolitan Museum of Art. "Are you planning on going?"

"I wouldn't miss it," I said. "I need to get tickets." Impressionist art was a passion of mine.

"You should really wait to go. The gallery was packed today. It was quite difficult to move about."

She put the teapot and cups on a tray and carried them into the living room. "Would you mind bringing the flowers, Irina."

Tricia placed the tray on the end of coffee table, then took the flowers from me and put the vase in the center of the table. Alice, coming in from the kitchen with a watering can, proceeded to water the plants on the tables in front of their tall windows. I counted six plants on the tables.

I went over to Alice attempting a conversation. "I recognize a few of the plants. What are you growing?"

"Different types of herbal plants," Tricia said from over on the sofa.

I should have known, herbs.

"Irina, I have a Degas book I brought home today from work you may be interested in."

I went over and sat down on their stark white sofa next to Tricia. Their decorating style was modern, clean lines, bare surfaces, abstract art on the walls. The ceilings had been lowered, covering the ornate crown molding, medallions, and cornices that I had in my apartment. I couldn't imagine why anyone would want to eradicate the architectural details of these grand historic landmarks.

Tricia handed me the book and I paged through it while she poured the tea.

I stopped looking when I came upon one of Degas' dance paintings. "Stephen didn't look well at all. His coloring was poor. He should see a doctor." I knew I was being repetitious, but I was truly concerned about Stephen.

Alice glanced over with a fake smirk. "It's the middle of winter. Everyone one looks pale. You look pale."

"Did you teach ballet today?" Tricia asked, changing the subject. She held out the cup and saucer. "Degas' dancing paintings are so happy."

I smiled and nodded. "This is a lovely book." I closed the book and placed it on the table, accepting the tea set from Tricia.

"Do you think your young students will go on to be ballet dancers," Tricia asked.

"I can teach them the basics, challenge and encourage them. I'm sure many never will, but at least they'll have poise and confidence. Of course, I hope some will continue with their lessons."

Alice finished watering the plants and turned towards us, pushing her dark, wavy hair away from her eyes. "Tricia tells me your mother was a ballerina in Eastern Europe during the Cold War."

"She was. She danced with the Lithuanian National Opera and Ballet Theatre in Vilnius." I attempted a sip of my tea. Still too hot. "My parents emigrated from Lithuania in the late-1940s when the Soviets occupied the country. During that time many artists fled to go to the West. She joined the American Ballet Theatre here."

"What did your father do in Lithuania?" Alice asked.

"He was in shipping. They bought this brownstone soon after they arrived."

Tricia took a sip of her tea, then put her cup down. "Irina, do you ever miss dancing?"

"That was so long ago." I took a sip. The herb in the tea was definitely mint. "I had my day in the spotlight, a wonderful career as a soloist, and retired when I approached thirty-five."

"That's quite late for a dancer," Tricia said.

I put my teacup and saucer on the coffee table. "It is. The travelling and dancing abroad was great, but I've been teaching for over twenty years and I love that."

"Your parent's story would make an intriguing background for a mystery book," Alice said with a rare smile.

That seemed to come out of left field, both the smile and the interest for a mystery.

"Perhaps sometime I could interview you about them."

Alice was a mystery writer. She wasn't anywhere near being on The New York Times Best Sellers list, but she was successful in her own right. I had read one of her novels and found it actually quite disturbing. I wasn't sure I would want her writing a mystery based on my parents' background. I inwardly cringed thinking about it.

Her brow furrowed. "You know spies, espionage, that sort of thing."

"Are you working on a murder mystery now?"

Alice glanced over at Tricia. "Always. I'm working on the concept for one. I just came home from the library doing research for it."

"What's it about?" I asked.

She turned back to her plants picking off a few dead leaves. "Still fleshing out the details. I'd rather not say." Alice started for the kitchen. "Tricia, when is Stephen coming home? We probably should start getting dinner ready."

Well, that was abrupt, but then tact was never Alice's forte.

"In a couple of hours," Tricia responded.

While I finished my tea, Alice returned with a knife and proceeded to cut a few sprigs off of a plant with broad leaves that I didn't recognize and wasn't told the name of when I asked.

I stood up and collected my cup and sauce.

Tricia smiled. "That's fine, Irina, just leave it. I'll clean up later."

"Thank you for the tea and think about what I said."

Tricia had a blank look on her face.

"Regarding the doctor. For Stephen."

Alice grimaced and looked over at me with eyes that said, mind your own business.

Tricia went into the front closet and handed me my coat and bag. "Thank you again for the lovely flowers. That was so thoughtful of you."

I smiled, then walked across the hallway to my apartment and unlocked it. The second I opened the door and stepped inside, my apartment's warmth greeted me. Instantly I felt relief. I loved everything about my home, from the natural woodwork and colored walls to the high, plastered ceilings with exquisite, ten-inch crown moldings. After being in Tricia's home with all straight lines and sharp edges, this was incredibly cozy, a home with personality, soul.

The low sun in the floor-to-ceiling windows, hit my brightly colored, scarlet and gold, floral pillows on the sofa and my faded Persian carpet. I turned on some Vivaldi, then went into my bedroom to put my ballet things away. I took my hair out of the bun and brushed it out. In a decorative bowl near my bed sat four silver bangles. After slipping three on one wrist and one on the other, I went into the closet and chose a floral Anna Coroneo silk scarf for around my neck.

Finally comfortable, I turned on a lamp on a side table. Then sat in a favorite vintage chair in my colorful, bohemian living room and let out a long sigh. I loved old pieces, each had their own story. I picked up my mystery book from the table, then glanced around. Well-thumbed tomes lined my walls along with an extensive jazz and classical record collection. Personal photographs were atop tables and the fireplace mantle. To hell with feng shui, this was my abode.

Alice had cut herbs for dinner, should I also have an herbal garden? There was plenty of sunlight in the afternoon, even in the winter. I had several plants and loved caring for them, watching them grow. In a way, they imparted a feeling of hope. But I didn't have fresh herbs. Of course fresh herbs were abundant at the markets, even organic ones.

I glanced at my watch after having read for a while. Six o'clock. Finishing the chapter, I put my book back down on the table.

Looking forward to a peaceful evening at home, perhaps watching a movie, I walked onto the scarred pine floors of my kitchen. The room was somewhat small, but well equipped. I turned on the oven, then went into the refrigerator to get out the eggplant lasagna and the garlic bread I had made the previous evening. Popping both in the oven, I could almost immediately smell the good oil and fresh ingredients. Cooking always gave me a feeling of stability, of being grounded, indulging in a pleasure. And in a way, an act of love.

After making a green salad to go along with the lasagna, I uncorked a bottle of Cabernet Sauvignon, poured myself a glass, then sat at my small kitchen table to eat in front of my bright window. Last summer I had painted the window molding a bold yellow color. A touch of sunshine all year round. I smiled. Vivaldi streamed in from the speakers in the walls.

I had been studying mindfulness and an easy way to practice was during my meals. I planted my feet flat on the floor and checked my posture. I held the glass of wine up and noted the color and clarity. Then I swirled the wine, allowing oxygen to permeate it, and sniffed it before taking a sip. I took a bite of the lasagna, noting the texture, the aroma of fresh garlic and spices, the great flavor, tuning out any external stimuli or thoughts, concentrating only on the meal at hand. Lasagna...

What was wrong with Stephen? Strange that Tricia didn't take notice when Stephen's deteriorating health was so obvious. And Alice denied it also. Perhaps they didn't see it; they were with him everyday. But, no one could be that clueless.

Oh, right, the lasagna...

Chapter Two

Valentine's Day

I knocked on Margarite's door just before six-thirty. She had called earlier in the afternoon suggesting we have a drink before leaving for the restaurant.

As I waited, Tricia and Stephen came out of their apartment. Tricia was dressed to the hilt, wearing a Carolina Herrera rose jacquard dress she had shown me previously. I was used to seeing Stephen looking sharp in impeccably cut suits. He was a successful advertising sales representative. This evening he was hunched over, his long wool coat baggy, giving the appearance of someone in dire straits.

"Happy Valentine's Day," I said, trying to sound spirited while still studying Stephen. "Where are you going for dinner?"

Tricia stopped. Stephen was already at the front door and came back to us. "We haven't decided where to go yet," Tricia said in a disgusted voice, putting on her black wool coat.

"Margarite and I are going to Little Delhi. Their food is excellent."

Tricia looked at Stephen. "We love Little Delhi. Maybe we should go there."

He shrugged. "Sure. Doesn't matter. Although there will probably be a long wait."

"There will be a wait anywhere *without a reservation,*" she said.

Margarite opened the door, looked between us and smiled. "Hello, everyone."

When working, Margarite had a classic, stylish look, similar to what I would wear. Outside of work she liked to dress trendy, very-in-the-moment fashions, that perhaps were too trendy for her age. Of course, who was I to judge?

This evening she was wearing a bright teal above-the-knee flounce hem dress. A "personality dress" Margarite would call it, with over-the-knee boots and big earrings.

I turned back to Tricia and Stephen. "Well, wherever you decide, I hope you have a wonderful evening."

They started for the door. I heard Tricia say, "We should have made reservations *somewhere.*"

I looked at Margarite and raised my eyebrows.

"Come in."

I followed her into the living room. "New earrings?" I had seen the teal dress and boots previously.

She smiled. "Bling is back."

Margarite took my coat from my arm. "You look great, stunning really," she said looking at my knee-length, black and white color block dress.

On occasion Margarite had mentioned my style not being daring enough when out on the town.

"I just opened a bottle of Pinot Noir. I could use a glass about now." She took her reading glasses from the top of her head and put them on a table in the corner of her living room next to a pile of papers.

Margarite didn't quite seem her exuberant, energetic self. "Rough day?"

Margarite was a high school English teacher at a renowned neighborhood school on the Upper West Side. "I've been reading essays all day and still haven't recovered from the parent-teacher meetings earlier this week. After school today I went to yoga, but nothing releases you as well as a drink."

I stepped back for a second at her statement. "Doesn't yoga feel meditative?"

She laughed. "I pretty much just like wearing the flattering yoga pants. Besides a drink can awaken one's chakra just as well."

Margarite poured the wine while I looked around her apartment. She went more for the modern look as did Tricia and Stephen. Staying with neutrals and whites, her room still had crown moldings like mine around its high ceiling and unlike mine, all of the woodwork was painted white. Gypsy, Margarite's white and black tabby cautiously peeked around the corner, then weaved between us and disappeared under a chair.

Margarite put my glass of wine on the Lucite cocktail table, next to a large vase of gorgeous red roses, the only bright color in the room other than her dress and a couple of splashes on abstract oil paintings on the walls.

I sat down on a love seat and picked up the glass, took a sip, then motioned towards the flowers. "An admirer?" Slyly, I tried to count them. About ten years ago, Margarite had divorced her husband, a well-to-do lawyer, who had a wandering eye and trouble keeping his pants zipped. She had her emotional ups and downs due to his infidelities, but came out of the marriage well financially and received her apartment in the settlement. After the divorce many of her friends dropped her even though she was the one of the two everyone liked most.

She saw me eyeing the flowers and smiled. She had a radiant glow. "There are two dozen and I bought them for myself. I made a list yesterday of all the reasons I loved myself and figured I deserved them."

I laughed. "Hmm. A sort of gratitude list."

"You could say that."

"Did you embrace all of your weird habits?"

She laughed. "Of course. Self-love is important. You were on it."

I smiled. "As a weird habit or for being a terrific friend?"

She smiled again and took a drink of her wine. "By the way, talking about friends, Jerome called a little while ago to make sure we were still meeting him this evening. He said he might be a little late."

I laughed and shook my head. "What? He talked to you as well. And a little late? He's the one who was insistent on this meeting. I wonder why he called you. He had already talked to me about getting together."

"He's my friend too."

"I don't know what he's up to. Did he say anything else?"

"No!" she said abruptly in an unconvincing manner.

Perhaps Valentine's Day inspired strange behavior in some people, especially my friends.

Taking another sip of wine, I glanced at my watch. It was almost seven o'clock. "We'll have to get going. Our reservations are soon and I'm starving."

"Sounds good."

I stood up. "I'll be right back. Have you heard, there's been a rash of burglaries in the neighborhood? I want to double-check that I locked my door."

* * * *

After entering the dimly lit restaurant, we were greeted and soon shown to a table by the window. The restaurant was crowded, with most of the tables filled with couples. A lit candle sat in the center of the table. It was a romantic venue to bring a date.

We ordered a glass of wine, samosas, and the tandoori sample platter for appetizers. While we waited, I looked out the floor-to-ceiling window.

"Did you see Tricia and Stephen waiting for a table on the way in?" Margarite asked.

"I didn't." I glanced towards the entrance. "I'm sure they will have a long wait. There's quite the crowd."

I looked out the window again, then back at Margarite. I didn't want to be bad company.

"Is something bothering you, Irina? You look a bit down."

"I'm fine."

She squinted her eyes. "You're not fine. What's up?"

My shoulders tensed. "Nothing really."

"Come on, Irina. This is me you're talking to," Margarite said in a sing-song voice.

I hesitated. "I was thinking earlier today about a different Valentine's I spent with Robert."

"Your love from college."

I nodded. "Yes. We were in love. It was on a weekend like this, during my first year at NYU, that Robert and I moved into a small apartment in the Village." I glanced over to the table next to us, a couple was holding hands. "We were incredibly happy in our little apartment for four years."

"I thought you dropped out of school."

"I did after the first year of college, but we still lived together. At the beginning, I thought I could handle an art history degree and continue my ballet training. There wasn't enough time to do both well between dance classes and auditions. It was one or the other."

Our drinks arrived. I took a sip of the wine and put the glass down. "After Robert graduated, he moved to San Francisco. He said I didn't have enough time for him with my rigorous training, and truthfully I didn't have much, but what I had, I spent with him. I thought that was enough."

"That sounds pretty needy."

Our appetizers arrived, each looking like a work of art. I took a couple of shrimp off the platter and put them on my plate. After taking a bite, I put my fork back down.

25

Margarite chose a samosa. "Sounds like a complete loser. At least then...perhaps he's changed. People do change, you know. But he shouldn't have walked away so easily."

I squinted my eyes at her. "Well, it's all water under the bridge. I love my life here and my friends."

Margarite raised her glass. "Let's have a toast...to no regrets and to best friends celebrating Valentine's with each other."

We clinked our glasses together.

After the appetizers we ordered our entrées: Lamb Tikka for Margarite and the Chicken Manglorean for myself. When the food arrived, a plate of garlic naan was placed on the table. My chicken breast was smothered in green chilies, ginger and fresh curry leaves. It had an outstanding flavor.

After taking my first bite, I looked further into the restaurant and saw Stephen and Tricia now seated, both looking at menus, not talking. "Tricia and Stephen are about four tables from us." I slightly nodded. "To my right. At three o'clock."

Margarite stretched her neck to look at them. "Tricia looks fit to be tied. Did you see that scowl?"

"I hope they've made an appointment for Stephen at his doctor's," I said.

"He looks terrible. Do you hear him arguing with Alice all the time?" Margarite asked.

My forehead wrinkled. "You mean Tricia, right?"

"No. Alice. It was a bad idea to let her move in with them."

I nodded. "She's an odd one."

"You have to be odd to write the things she does. Have you read 'The Wrong End of the Street?'"

I laughed. "Not that one, but the novel I read was pretty dark." I took another bite of chicken and thought about the incredible taste. "Manhattan's expensive. Living with Tricia and Stephen might be the only way she can afford to be here."

Margarite shrugged her shoulders. "It's taking a toll on their marriage."

"You can see that and I can see that. I wonder if Tricia and Stephen can."

After declining dessert, I glanced over to Stephen and Tricia. While Tricia was eating, Stephen pushed his food around on his plate with his fork. It looked as if he hadn't even started yet.

We left just after nine-thirty and walked the two blocks to the Vanguard. The place was cozy, the lighting warm. It had brick walls, globe chandeliers, and was laid back, nothing pretentious about it. Jerome was no where in sight. We found a table and ordered a coffee and visited while we waited.

Just before ten o'clock Jerome walked through the door looking slightly frayed around the edges, brushing snow off of his buff brown corduroy jacket. Someone was in tow. A handsome, distinguished looking man with a wistful look on his face. There was something about the way he carried himself. I looked into his deep-set eyes.

My heart raced. "Robert," I whispered.

"Excuse me?" Margarite said, giving me a questioning look that was both sincere and not.

"It's Robert," I said biting my lip.

Jerome and Robert made their way over to our table.

"Surprise!" Jerome said, smiling large.

I was dumbstruck. I couldn't speak. I could feel Margarite looking over at me.

"Irina, aren't you going to say anything?" Jerome asked.

I felt like asking Jerome if he had any last words. I wanted to strangle him.

Robert bent over and kissed me on my cheek. I could feel his warmth.

"Hello, Irina. Nice to see you again." He had a self-assured look about him.

"Rob...bert." I wanted to kick myself for stuttering. Then I looked from Jerome to Margarite back to Robert again. "This is quite the surprise."

Feeling my face turn red, I turned to Margarite and introduced her to Robert.

"So here you are. I finally get to meet you." She giggled.

Her response would have been funny if this situation was, which it wasn't. What had possessed Jerome? What was he thinking? He could have at least warned me. I realized then that Margarite had been in on it as well. Jerome would have had to tell her to make sure we showed up.

The only thing I could think of or manage to say was, "Please sit down."

After they sat down, Jerome let out a sigh putting his suede patched elbows on the table. "Isn't this just like our college days?" Jerome said, with a playful gleam in his eyes. He then looked over at Margarite. "Minus Margarite...of course."

Obviously, Jerome enjoyed being in this moment. I didn't know how to act, what to say. My glare moved from him and softened when I glanced over at Robert. He had hardly changed at all physically, other than his thick hair was graying. His beard still had a bit of brown in it. He had the same bright blue sparkling eyes. Robert looked down for a few seconds. His skin was lined and tanned like he had just visited a warm country. His dress was casual: navy cashmere sweater, button down shirt. Old feelings awakened that belonged to two people forty years ago.

"Irina, it's really great to see you again. Silver hair becomes you. You're just as lovely as you were in college."

My eyes widened. "What brings you to New York, Robert?"

"To be honest, I came to see you."

I swallowed and had absolutely no response to that. Of course, I didn't believe what he had said. No one would come to New York just to see an old love. Still it was flattering to hear the words.

Jerome stood up. "Margarite, I'd like to show you a favorite abstract of mine. It's over by the bar." He put his hand on her arm as if to help her up.

"We can see it later, don't you think?" She looked over at me.

I motioned as discreetly as I could with my head to have her follow Jerome. I wanted to learn why Robert was really here.

They left, Jerome talking animatedly as they made their way to the next room.

Robert kept steady eye contact on me. He moved his hand towards me, then withdrew it, and put it on his lap. "Irina, I've been thinking a lot about you these past several months."

I took a deep breath. "I heard that Samantha died last year. I'm so sorry."

"Too young. She had a long battle with breast cancer." He shook his head. "Thank you. We have two sons."

"So I've heard."

At that moment there was a disruption at a nearby table. A young man stood up, slamming his chair against the table. "I'm through with you. I've never been a priority." He grabbed his coat and stormed out of the restaurant. The young woman crying, threw some bills on the table and followed him out the door.

"You do look great. Your blue eyes that sparkle, I've missed those. I followed your career you know."

I looked from the retreating woman back to Robert.

Robert told me Jerome had filled him in on what was going on in my life. He had told him I wasn't with anyone. He knew about my parents and said he was sorry about their passing.

As he continued talking, Margarite headed back to the table. "Irina, have you ever looked at the art work here? It's phenomenal."

I glanced up at a modern art painting on the wall overhead and then at Robert. He at me.

"Did I interrupt...?" Margarite said.

Jerome then returned with a waiter carrying a bottle of champagne and four glasses. "I thought a toast was in order. Now that you two are back together." Jerome looked at me with mischievous expectation.

I raised my eyebrows.

After the waiter filled the glasses, Jerome held his up, "To renewing old friendships, old romances."

I smiled, picturing my hands now loosening my grip around Jerome's neck, but still not completely. I was upset for him not telling me about Robert ahead of time.

Robert looked over at Margarite. "And to new friends."

We clinked our glasses. Still visualizing, I took a sip and looked over my glass at Robert. He smiled at me. Bubbles tickled my nose.

Margarite put her glass down. "Is it true, Robert, you were trying to date Irina at NYU and she always refused...until of course..."

"More like pestering," Jerome laughed. "He was relentless. He finally wore her down and won her heart."

Awkward.

"Irina, I heard someone mention there's a new exhibit at The Met," Robert said. "Would you be interested in going?"

Margarite interrupted. "Irina and I have tickets to see Swan Lake tomorrow evening, but something has come up. I can't make it."

I looked at Margarite. "We've been looking forward to this ballet for months. What could have possibly come up so suddenly?"

She shrugged.

"It would be *a shame* to have the ticket go to waste," Jerome said looking at Robert.

Jerome was so transparent.

"Irina, I'd love to go to the performance with you," Robert said.

Beyond awkward. I looked between Robert, Jerome, and Margarite. Hopeful faces stared back at me. What was this? Some kind of conspiracy?

I took another sip of the champagne and put my glass down. "Sure. Why not?"

Chapter Three

Sunday, February 15

I opened my apartment door to find Margarite standing there with a smug look on her face. "Well, Irina, now that you've slept on it, what do you think?"

I looked past her, up and down the hall. "You'd better come in," I snickered. "I don't want to have the neighbors hear me on the top floor."

Margarite raised her eyebrows and smirked.

I closed the door, then folded my arms. "Have you *lost your mind*? I still can't understand how you could do that."

She smiled. "Do what?"

"You know. Not telling me about Robert ahead of time. You're *supposed* to be my best friend."

"And spoil the surprise. What do you mean, *supposed*?"

I shook my head slightly. I knew what Margarite was trying to do. "You should know then I don't like surprises like *that*."

"Well, didn't you like seeing Robert?"

I could feel my heartbeat quicken at the sound of his name, but didn't say anything, then smiled.

She let out a deep, gratifying sigh. "See!"

"But then giving up your seat to Swan Lake?"

"A small sacrifice. You'll be in your element at the ballet."

I put my arm around Margarite's shoulder.

"Oh...Margarite. Would you like a cup of coffee?"

"I thought you'd never ask." She followed me into the kitchen. "By the way, you never told me how good looking Robert is. Quite distinguished looking."

I moved the newspaper off the kitchen chair so Margarite could sit down.

Margarite clicked her tongue. "Irina, sometimes you don't know what's best for you. You're becoming a Puritan. You haven't been with anyone for a while now."

I waited for Margarite to finish her little rant, shrugged, then said. "I'm quite happy with the way things are, thank you. By the way, please keep tomorrow evening open for dinner. I'd like to make it up to you for giving away your ticket."

Margarite smiled. "Of course. So tell me, what are you wearing this evening?"

I rolled my eyes.

"Make sure it's something irresistible."

I smiled. "Robert was handsome, wasn't he?"

* * * *

He put his empty plate on the coffee table. "The spanakopita was delicious," Robert said, dabbing his mouth with a napkin.

"I'm glad you liked it. I figured we should have a little something before the ballet to hold us over." I passed Robert the plate of crab stuffed mushrooms."

"No, no," Robert said, putting his hands out in refusal. "I'm fine. I've had enough, thank you." He put his napkin next to his plate. "After the performance, I thought we could go out for dinner. I've heard of a great little intimate restaurant close to the theater."

Perhaps he'd tell me then why he was really in New York City. "Where do you think you might look for an apartment?"

"I'm over by Riverside Boulevard. I'm renting an apartment there."

So he hadn't just arrived in Manhattan. It took a while to get into an apartment. That kills his theory about coming to see me. How long had he been here?

* * * *

While locking the door to my apartment, Stephen and Tricia came in the front door. Stephen was looking a bit better this evening. Perhaps it took two days of the weekend to rest up from the pressures of his job. Before I had a chance to make introductions, I thought I saw a glint of recognition in both Stephen and Robert. Had they known each other before? Neither of them said anything.

We took a taxi over to Lincoln Center and walked towards the State Theater. The striking Revson Fountain in the plaza and the magnificent architecture of the theater were gorgeous. There was something about how Lincoln Center glowed in the evening that made me feel so alive. I never took this breathtaking cultural center for granted or tired of seeing it. People walked through the open area at all times of the night. It made for quite the romantic stroll even in winter months.

We entered the imposing State Theater located on the south side of the main plaza. It was one of the most beautiful theaters I had ever performed in. The Promenade featured many works of modern art. As we were led to our seats in center orchestra, I looked up at the massive spherical chandelier in the center of the gold-latticed ceiling.

"This reminds me of when we went to performances in college," Robert said, handsome in a dark suit, with his graying hair all tousled.

I smiled as we sat down. "Only we have better seats. No longer in the nosebleed section."

"At times I'd have vertigo." Robert laughed.

I laughed. "On the bright side, we were able to see the elaborate formations of the dancers."

"Irina, being in Manhattan has brought back many happy memories." He placed his hand on my leg.

I crossed my leg feeling uncomfortable with his hand there. I hoped he'd take the hint and cool it a little. "When I performed here, I'd get a thrill looking out at the audience, seeing the chicest, most designer-clad women in their evening gowns and men in immaculate suits."

Robert removed his hand and turned, looking at the attendees. "The clothing certainly has become more casual. Look over there. Those must be tourists. Showing up in jeans and sweatshirts. It takes a bit away from the atmosphere, wouldn't you say?"

I started looking at the program, reading the scenario of Swan Lake.

"These really are fabulous seats," Robert said.

Perhaps he was nervous, talking about the seats again. "Margarite and I have sat here before. It's the perfect balance of the view and acoustics."

"It's a shame Margarite had to bow out. I'll have to make it up to her."

I looked at him and wondered if he ever would. I hoped so. "Amazing she did. This was to be our big outing of the winter. Swan Lake has been sold out for months."

Robert turned and looked intently into my eyes. "Perhaps she thought it was important for us to be together. Irina, did you ever think about me, about us, over the years?"

I inwardly rolled my eyes. What nerve he had, but I answered anyway. "From time to time."

Robert sighed. "It was terrible the way I left, so sudden."

You have *that* right. I didn't respond.

His voice weakened. "I was young. We both were young."

The lights dimmed. "It's about to begin," I whispered.

Robert reached over and then put his hand on mine. I didn't remove it.

The curtain opened. I didn't know if I had goosebumps from Robert's hand on mine or the music beginning with its symphonic qualities. Most likely the latter. Magic lit the stage and beauty took flight. Soon I was captured and transported into another world. A world that I had danced in, on this very stage. The world belonging to Odette and Odile and Siegfried and Von Rothbart.

The ballet began with Prince Siegfried celebrating his birthday, interrupted by his mother, who was resigned that he should choose a wife at the Royal Ball the following evening.

Robert glanced in my direction and squeezed my hand.

I whispered, "The dancers are phenomenal. A perfect execution of movement and music."

Robert whispered back. "I love your enthusiasm and energy. I've always found that quite attractive."

Wow! He was coming on a bit strong. I refocused back to the ballet. As I watched, my mind wandered ahead to the later acts. I, too,would be horrified by the prince's betrayal as was Odette and would never put up with someone who professed his love for me and then went off with another to whom he also professed his love. I shook my head and turned my attention back to Act One.

In the second act, the Prince and his friends went on a hunt that evening, having seen swans. At the lake when the prince took aim at a swan, Odette transformed into a beautiful maiden. She revealed the spell that was cast on her and the other swans by the evil sorcerer Von Rothbart. I noted as Odette floated, barely touching the floor, she revealed a sensuous passion. The air was charged between the prince and the regal captive. Their Adagio had grace, exquisite fluidity, and heat. It made me, for some reason I couldn't understand, feel incredibly euphoric.

At intermission we decided to go out on the Promenade. As we stood in line for drinks, I looked around admiring the impressive space. The floors were inlaid travertine marble. I looked up at the gold leaf ceiling as we took our cocktails up a dramatic spiral stairway to the second floor balcony and looked out at the breathtaking fountain in the plaza. The sounds of a string quartet rose from the lobby.

Police Lieutenant Charles Whitney was also enjoying the view. He came over and joined us. Charles Whitney had presence. His eyes smiled at me before his mouth did. Smartly dressed wearing a whimsical paisley bow tie and a black suit, he and I often met up at the ballet and opera performances. An art aficionado and friend since my younger days, he often visited me at my performances both backstage and afterwards.

He and I exchanged greetings and I made introductions.

Charles began to grin. His brilliant white teeth shone brightly. "So you're Robert from Irina's college days. I've heard much about you."

Robert looked over at me and smiled. "Mostly good, I hope."

"Are you visiting or have you moved back?" Charles asked, not responding to Robert's remark.

I had the feeling that Robert was being sized up by Charles, his eyes penetrating Robert, assessing, dissecting.

Robert gave my arm a squeeze. "I recently came back. Missed close friends and Manhattan."

Charles tilted his head to the side, arched an eyebrow, looking at me.

Feeling my face blush and my heart beat faster, I asked Charles, "Are you enjoying Swan Lake?"

"Something's missing from it. Hmm. I can't quite put my finger on it." A teasing smile appeared on Charles' face. He stroked his chin. "Oh, yes, seeing *you* in it. I can still picture you up on stage." He looked over at Robert. "Totally ravishing, of course." He held out his hands to mine. I took his. "Irina captivated the hearts of the audience including my own."

I blushed further. It had been a while since anyone had mentioned anything similar about my performances. "Oh Charles. You're sweet. Flattery will get you everywhere."

Charles gave me a peck on the cheek and looked down at his watch, having let loose of my hands. "Better get back to our seats. It was interesting meeting you, Robert." He looked at me and slightly raised his eyebrows again as he turned to leave.

"Yes. It was interesting to meet you as well," Robert responded after him without smiling.

We returned to our seats. I picked up my program and started looking at what companies the dancers had been with.

Robert looked at his program then turned to me. "Do you and Charles have a history?"

Surprised by his question, I looked at him speechless.

"I mean have you dated?"

Still a bit shocked by his questions and annoyed in a way, he had been gone for forty years, I continued to study Robert for a few more moments. "Charles and I are good friends. We're quite fond of each other. Yes, we've gone out on occasion."

Robert wrinkled his brow, then looked straight ahead, pursing his lips. I went back to my program.

After a couple of minutes he said, "He seemed more than a bit enamored with you."

I rustled my program a bit. "Let's drop it."

The lights dimmed and the story of evil and trickery, glamour, infatuation and faithfulness continued. Oh, yes, and the search for true love, all amidst the beautiful choreography.

The third act opened with the guests arriving at the palace for the Ball as well as a disguised Von Rathbart with his enchantress daughter Odile, transformed to look like Odette.

The prince had eyes only for her and responded with ecstatic jetés, very well executed.

Although Odile was cool, mysterious, and even disturbing, she was the ultimate seductress. "What perfect double fouettés," I whispered to Robert. Then Odile turned her arms out and held them high in the effect of a lifted wing. "Perfect!" I said under my breath. After Siegfried realized his mistake, he returned to the lake in search of Odette.

In the final act, Odette, distressed by Siegfried's disloyalty, resigned herself to death. Upon returning to Odette, Siegfried apologized. Von Rathbart appeared insistent on Siegfried keeping his pledge to marry his daughter, which would result in Odette remaining a swan forever. Siegfried and Odette leaped into the lake, choosing to die together. Von Rathbart lost his power, died, and in doing so released his power over the other swans.

After the final bows were taken, Robert exclaimed, "What a spectacular performance!"

"Yes it was. Truly magnificent."

While we waited at the coat check, Robert suggested dinner again at the new upscale restaurant a friend had told him about.

"Do you know what I'm really hungry for?" I said.

"Just mention it. We'll go to any restaurant you'd like."

"A cheeseburger."

Robert's eyes widened giving an incredulous stare. "What? A cheeseburger? Don't you think burgers are a bit too lowbrow after a ballet?"

"Nonsense. I know this hidden treasure, a great diner nearby that has the best burgers and milkshakes, not to mention their onion rings. The locals flock to it."

He leaned in. "Sounds like something a ballerina would want!" Robert said in a still disbelieving voice. "Aren't we a bit overdressed?"

I looked down at my black ruffled sheath dress. "It'll be fine. Besides there's something fun about eating burgers in formal-wear."

Robert laughed, his eyes warm with admiration. "Irina, this is one of many things I love about you. Still a non-conformist. Okay, lets go."

I smiled. Love? I'd need to be cautious. He had been coming on a bit too strong this entire evening.

* * * *

"They've forgotten about us, Irina. Our waiter may never return, *ever*."

"It will be worth the wait." I looked up at the large clock on the wall. It had been a while.

"It has been almost an hour since we placed our order and still nothing. No drinks, no silverware, nada. Is this how it usually is?"

The diner was half empty. It reminded me of being on a movie set from the 1970s. The counter and bright orange booths were old school with brassy, vintage light fixtures hanging from the ceiling. Dark wood paneling covered the walls. The linoleum floors shined like they were new. I shrugged my shoulders and smiled. "I don't come that often."

Robert went on. "I think 'Manhattan's Most Delish' should be your former favorite hidden treasure."

I laughed. "You should have eaten the stuffed mushrooms."

Robert pinched his lips together. "I'm trying to be on my best behavior, but how long will we have to wait?" He looked towards the kitchen.

I was about to wave down a waiter, any waiter, to see what was going on, when ours flew out of the kitchen carrying a huge tray towards us.

He plopped the tray in front of us and said in a loud voice, "What can I say? The cook got your order mixed up with someone else's."

Robert gave a disgusted look.

I looked at our plates. I had ordered the Manhattan's Most Delish burger with feta and extra onions, Robert, the Muenster burger with an order of onion rings.

We both dug in and ate for a couple of minutes without talking. The taste was incredible.

I was concentrating on the different flavors when Robert said, "I must admit this is good."

I looked up, then took a sip of my chocolate shake. "Good?"

"Okay, great."

"Told you."

Robert laughed. "Still not sure it was worth the wait."

"You're incorrigible." I took another bite of my burger. A bit of grease dripped on my chin.

Robert took his napkin off his lap, reached across the table, and gently dabbed my chin, a bit more thoroughly than necessary, then moved up to my lips. "I thought ballet dancers were pressured to maintain a certain weight, watch what they ate."

Note to self. Obsessive napkin user and calorie counter.

I raised my eyebrows, ignored his remark, then padded my mouth with my own napkin. "Thanks. Robert, tell me about your sons. What are their ages?"

He put his napkin back on his lap and reached for another onion ring. A flush crept across his cheeks and his ears turned red. "It's warm in here."

I hadn't noticed. "Your sons?"

"I'm so proud of them. Theo's the oldest. He's a civil engineer. And John's an architect. Large buildings, landmark buildings. Skyscrapers."

"How old are—"

Robert shifted in his chair, then interrupted me. "I so enjoy this evening being with you. What about going out tomorrow, Irina?"

41

The waiter brought over the check. Robert took out his credit card.

"Cash only," he said and left.

"Of course. I should have known." He opened his wallet and grimaced.

"I'll get this."

"How about tomorrow?"

"I have class and promised Margarite she and I would get together for dinner to make up for her giving you this evening's ticket. She was so kind to have given you her ticket." Perhaps he would offer to pay for dinner. "Do you have some project you're working on in Manhattan?" Something?

"I thought Margarite couldn't make it to the ballet."

"Why have you come back to Manhattan, Robert?"

He leaned over and kissed my cheek. "I've already told you. The next day, then?"

"We'll have plenty of opportunities now that you'll be here for a while."

Chapter Four

That morning as I left my apartment to go to Margarite's, I ran into Stephen. He was in the hallway outside his apartment having a hard time trying to put a brown paper sack into his already full overnight bag. He looked up, his eyes glassy, saw me and nodded. I smiled, but was taken aback by how ill he looked again, even worse than a few days previous. What had happened since yesterday evening? His skin had a sickly pallor, a bluish tinge. I offered to help him since his hands were shaking.

"These damn drinks. I don't know why Tricia insists on my taking all of these herbal concoctions of hers?"

They certainly weren't working. "Just being a good wife. She's concerned about your health."

His forehead wrinkled. "Thanks for helping me."

"Are you going out of town?"

"Yes. A colleague is picking me up to take me to the airport. I have a conference and Tricia had a previous engagement. She couldn't take me."

"Stephen, do you think you'll even get that container past airport security?"

"I'll either drink it on the way or dump it when I get there. Don't tell Tricia." He half-smiled. "I better get going."

"So, you're not going alone." That was good. The way he's been looking lately, he shouldn't be travelling alone.

"Oh, he's not going to the conference. Just giving me a lift to the airport."

There was a rap at the front door. I walked over and let the person in while Stephen fumbled with his bag.

He looked past me over to Stephen without even as much as a 'thank you.'

"Irina, this is Alex Rankin," Stephen said.

I looked into Alex's dark eyes and smiled. He clearly wasn't interested in chit-chat. I held out my hand to be polite. "Nice to meet you, Alex."

"Right. Same," he said unenthusiastically, then turned to Stephen. "We'd better get going."

"I hope you have a great trip."

"Thanks, Irina." Stephen forced another smile.

I knocked on Margarite's door watching them hustle through the front door, Alex leading the way.

"Come in. How was the ballet?"

I grimaced as Alex let the door slam on Stephen. Then I turned to Margarite and smiled thinking of Robert and the ballet and having burgers afterward dressed in our finery. "It was wonderful."

Margarite closed the door and started for the dining room, asking over her shoulders, "Did Robert tell you why he decided to grace you with his presence?"

I wrinkled my brow. "You gave him the ticket."

She stopped. "I meant in Manhattan."

I shrugged. "He claims it's to see me."

Continuing to follow Margarite, I told her about the evening's events and raised my eyebrows when I noticed her table set for four.

"I didn't think you would mind that I invited Tricia and Alice as well. Both were free this morning and I know you wanted to learn more about Stephen's health and Tricia's well being."

"That's fine."

Margarite took some cloth napkins out of her buffet. "And you believe that Robert's in Manhattan just to see you."

"I don't know what to believe," I said, watching Margarite fold napkins in a fan shape. "And Robert's moved here." I told her where he was living.

"On the way over, I saw Stephen leaving his apartment. He looked like death had definitely warmed over. A *charming* friend was giving him a ride to the airport. He said Tricia had an engagement. Guess that was you."

She finished folding the last napkin. "Charming? Really?"

I rolled my eyes. "I was being sarcastic. He was anything but. No one you would be interested in."

"Too bad." She put the napkins on the plates.

"It's hard to believe Tricia would allow Stephen to travel in his condition."

The doorbell rang. Margarite headed for the kitchen. "Irina could you please answer the door?"

Tricia and Alice looked jovial. A noticeable change in Alice. She carried a plate of different kinds of breads.

"Those look delicious. How nice you both have the morning off."

"I have the entire day. I was lucky to get away," Tricia said, "especially with the exhibit going on."

Alice laughed. "Sister time! And to catch up on cooking."

I didn't get the joke. I closed the door.

"I saw Stephen leaving earlier with his friend. He looked even worse than the other day when I came over." No use beating around the bush.

Alice's eyes narrowed. "You sure keep tabs on everyone."

Margarite came into the living room. "It's important for all of us to watch out for each other. Glad you could both make it."

"Did Stephen ever call the doctor?" I asked.

"No. I told him you were concerned about his health, but he felt whatever he had was passing," Tricia said.

I raised my eyebrows.

"He'll be in Miami for a couple of days," Tricia added.

I wish Tricia had taken a few days off to have gone with Stephen to Miami. He shouldn't have been away by himself with the way he looked. Why didn't Tricia seem worried? She seemed so nonchalant about the whole thing.

Alice handed the plate to Margarite. "Looking forward to going to our favorite restaurants," Alice said.

"I thought you were going to catch up with cooking," I said.

"Irina, we're busy during the week. We make meals ahead," Tricia said. She turned to Margarite. "And we plan on seeing a couple of plays."

"Tricia, do you think Stephen should have gone to Miami alone?"

Alice didn't give Tricia any time to answer my question. "I tried to talk Tricia into taking a few days off while Stephen was gone, to go someplace warmer also, but with the exhibition on, she didn't think she could get away that long. We'll have plenty of time to travel—"

Tricia quickly added, "when the weather gets nicer."

Plenty of time to travel? It sounded like they were planning to travel without Stephen. What was going on here?

Margarite smiled looking between them and me. "Everything's ready."

We followed Margarite to the dining room. She placed Alice's plate of bread next to a gorgeous arrangement of daffodils, tulips, and irises in the center of the table. We sat down. Margarite had made mimosas and handed us each a glass.

While we sipped our drinks, Margarite served us a piece of a lovely vegetable strata. I put down my glass, took a bite, and closed my eyes. The blend of the different cheeses was exquisite.

I heard a loud clink of a glass against the plate. "We're thinking of going to Paris," Alice said. "Paris in spring doesn't that sound wonderful?"

I looked at Tricia. "Will Stephen be able to get away with his busy schedule?"

"It sounds romantic," Margarite said. "I've been there with a lover or two in the springtime. Oh, and with my ex-husband also." She laughed.

"Irina, have you ever danced in Paris?" Tricia asked, not answering my question about Stephen.

After taking a sip of my drink, I smiled. "Oui, certainement! Some of the happiest times of my career were in Europe," I said, then looked down. And the saddest. When I looked up I saw Margarite give me a questioning look. "I danced in soloist roles at Opéra de Paris with my company. The Europeans loved us. We 'sang' to them with our movements and made them weep." I laughed. "Lots of blood, sweat, tears, and laughter, and often lavish parties afterwards."

I took a bite of Alice's breakfast bread. It tasted strongly on herbs. I raised my eyebrows. Stephen wasn't the only one getting herbs. I put it down and took a forkful of the delicious strata to try and get the strong taste out of my mouth. "What about Stephen? He—"

"How exciting," Tricia interrupted while buttering a piece of bread.

"Where else did you dance?" Alice asked.

Were they really interested or was this a ploy so I wouldn't continue talking about Stephen?

"Did you dance behind the Iron Curtain?" Alice continued.

"Yes, in Romania, Moscow, Warsaw, many others. I jumped at the opportunity to dance in Lithuania at the beginning of our six month tour. I wanted to see the country my parents were from. I thought perhaps I could even visit relatives."

"Did you?" Alice asked. She had hardly eaten any of her food.

"Finishing the piece of strata, I put my fork down. Alice certainly seemed interested. Had she started the book she talked about the last time we spoke, with her wanting background on my parents. Still she and Tricia were avoiding my question about Stephen's ability to travel. "No time when I was there." I glanced down at my watch. "Oh, my, talking about dancing, no time now. I must get ready for my ballet class."

"We should be off soon as well. We're going to see The Book of Mormon this afternoon." Tricia took a last bite of her bread.

I got up from the table. "I'll see myself out. Enjoy your day ladies and Margarite your day off from school. Thank you for the lovely brunch. Remember dinner tonight."

"Looking forward to it."

"You choose the place. I'll call you when I get home."

It was true I did have to rush off to get ready for class, but I couldn't take Tricia and Alice any longer. Clearly, they didn't see, or didn't want to see, the dangerous condition Stephen was in. Why didn't they, when it was so evident?

* * * *

"Dancers, it's time to warm up and stretch our muscles. We need to build our strength." I nodded to Jerome and he started playing one of Chopin's Nocturnes.

We sat in a circle. There were ten of us, We pointed our toes up and down then reached out and touched them, then laid all the way back, stretched, and sat back up with our arms over our heads. "Reach for the stars. Wonderful! Everyone up, but stay in the circle. Let's go around, starting with Molly, say and demonstrate your favorite dance step. Then we'll all imitate it."

When it was Ivy's turn, she went into second position, then smiled large. I returned her smile.

"Children, time for the barre. After, we'll do some center work and then I'll tell you about the pieces you will be performing for our spring recital."

Ivy and Molly started clapping.

I smiled.

"Will they be as much fun as The Sugar Plum Fairy," Molly asked.

Ivy nodded her head in agreement with another big smile.

I laughed. I loved seeing the children so excited. "Of course. That was lovely at the Christmas recital. Remember the standing ovation you received?"

On the way over to the barre, Ivy mentioned she had gotten pink ballet slippers just like mine.

"Now let's start with the basic barre exercises in first and second position. Facing the barre, releve in first position. Now we'll demi plie twice and grande plie once. For the battement tendu, starting with your right legs, everyone, point your feet and stretch as you slide your leg backwards, strike, and brush against the floor. Remember to keep your backs straight. Now to the center...the front."

After the exercises, while the children gathered in a circle, I glanced up at movement just outside of the window. The same man I had seen during the previous class looked in the window as he walked by. He was bundled up in a black woolen coat and winter hat, but I still recognized him. Who was this stranger? Was it a coincidence I kept seeing him?

"We will be working on two pieces for our recital. I think you'll enjoy them. The first is called Valse Lente from the

Ballet Coppélia." I smiled looking at the children wrinkling their noses. I had danced to Valse Lente at my first recital when I had started ballet at age eight. "And the second will be Swan Lake Act II – Cygnet's Dance. Dance of the Little Swans."

Ivy raised her hand instantly. "Miss Irina, may we wear flowers in our hair?"

"I don't see why not, Ivy. That would be lovely."

Another of the children raised his hand instantly.

"Yes, Corbin."

"I went to Swan Lake last night."

"Wasn't it beautiful?"

He giggled. "Yes."

"All right, first, we'll listen to Mr. Jerome play the music and then I'll demonstrate how we'll dance to it."

I stood up. "Children, we are the ultimate artists, creating our own masterpieces." The music began again. I danced with happy abandon, becoming aware of my body making contact with the floor, stretching, a tingling of a muscle. Mindfulness.

At the end of class, each child bowed or curtsied out of respect for the teacher as the others applauded. Molly came forward and performed the most beautiful curtsy. Ivy almost fell. I smiled inside. Ivy was so adorable. I wanted to give her a big hug.

After everyone had been picked up, Jerome asked me about Robert, smiling large. "So how is your boyfriend?"

I rolled my eyes. "Boyfriend? Get real. You sound so...so high school."

He smirked and batted his eyes. "You didn't know me in high school. Perhaps we could double-date soon. You and Robert, Anthony and I."

I laughed. "I don't think so. Jerome, why did Robert really come back to Manhattan after all this time? You've been talking with him over the years? You must know."

Jerome smiled. "Robert's crazy for you."

I crossed my arms and tapped my foot, staring at him.

Jerome's smile wavered. "Have you met up with Monica yet?"

"Monica? Monica, who?"

"You know Monica and Todd. You and Robert were friends with them in college."

I hesitated trying to picture them. "I'm drawing a blank. I don't remember them at all. We couldn't have been very good friends. What about Monica?"

Jerome's brows pulled in. He started packing up his things, avoiding eye contact. "Ask Robert about her."

* * * *

Margarite and I walked to Camellos, a nearby Italian restaurant and one of Margarite's favorites. As an appetizer we ordered the garlic spinach Fontina fondue. Margarite ordered Chicken and Asparagus Fettuccine. I ordered Eggplant Parmigiana.

"This garlic is intense. Good thing you don't have a hot date with Robert this evening."

Margarite and Jerome sounded so juvenile. I didn't feel like talking about Robert this evening. While I twirled the melted cheese on my cube of bread, I changed the subject and told Margarite about class and little Ivy and Molly.

"It's a shame you never had children. You love them so."

I looked down. My eyes started watering. Then a tear rolled down my cheek.

"I'm sorry, Irina? I didn't know children was a touchy subject."

Margarite was my best friend and I had held this secret for decades. "I did have a child. A son."

She looked at me and squinted. "You did? When? Where? With whom? Oh no, he died?"

I looked down at my plate. "It's a long story."

Margarite poured me another glass of wine. "Do you have another engagement? I don't. We have all evening."

I smiled. It would be good, no great, to tell my best friend about my son. I took a sip of wine.

"After a performance in Kaunas—"

"Lithuania?"

I nodded. "After my first performance in Kaunas, a young man, a student I was led to believe, waited for me to come out of the theatre. He asked if I wanted to get a cup of coffee and I agreed. After performances I normally socialized with the other dancers and choreographers, but I wanted to experience first-hand about Lithuania. Every evening that week, this young man waited for me. We had great conversations."

Margarite tilted her head to one side. "Did this young man have a name?"

"Vytautas. His name was Vytautas."

"Okay, continue."

I smiled. "We talked about music and art, literature, politics. There was a ban against printing in the Lithuanian language and when it was lifted many European literary movements occurred. One author that comes to mind that Vytautas and I both enjoyed was Vincas Kreve-Mickeviciusn. My father had read to me, actually translated some of his works."

Her eyes glazing over, Margarite poured herself more wine, took a sip, and then supported her head with her hand.

"Vytautas told me about the revolution going on. I told him about America, my family. On the sixth evening I was in Kaunas, instead of going to our little café, he took me back to his small apartment. His tiny kitchen was smaller than my bathroom at home. It was totally Bohemian, bookcases on every wall and art work, prints above the bookcases. Many were by—."

"And?"

"And, we made love. I stayed at his apartment that night, which of course was against the rules."

Margarite perked up and smiled. "Good for you. Did you get caught?"

"No. In the morning we said our goodbyes, promising to meet that evening at his apartment. It was to be my company's last evening in the city.

When I arrived back at the hotel, my roommate, a fellow dancer who had also socialized with the locals, told me my young man was actually a KGB agent."

Margarite put her fork down. "Unbelievable. You must have been heartbroken."

"Heartbroken and devastated. I thought he was a patriot, a revolutionary. He told me his name meant 'defender of the people.' My parents had fled Lithuania because of people like him and I had fallen for the worse of the lot. Questions started going through my mind that didn't make any sense, that I shouldn't have cared about. Had he truly fallen in love with me or perhaps thought I was a spy?"

"Irina, how could you have fallen in love with anyone in less than a week?"

I shook my head. "Well, I did. I never felt like that about anyone else, other than Robert."

Margarite's eyes went wide. She picked up her glass of wine and took another sip. "*Really?*"

"I didn't go to his apartment and returned straight to the hotel after the final performance. We left early the next morning for ....."

"Did you ever hear from him again?"

"No. Never. I stopped having my periods which had happened previously, because of being so physically active. So that didn't phase me."

"Didn't you have morning sickness?"

"Not at all. In my fourth month, I knew and went to the doctor and danced until my fifth month and then took a leave. I flew to France, to a friend's and stayed with her until I had the baby, a sweet boy, with blonde hair and blue eyes. I had already inquired about adoption and gave him up."

"That must have been hard."

I nodded. "The hardest thing I've ever done. I came home and two months after having the baby, I returned to the company for the remainder of my career. The artistic director was a good friend and I had already achieved a certain acclaim. He welcomed me back."

Margarite was quiet.

I picked up my glass and finished the wine. "So there you have it." I reached for another piece of bread. So did Margarite. We ate a few moments in silence.

"Did you have regrets?"

I put my fork down. "Of course. I laid in bed many nights agonizing if I had made the right decision. I still do sometimes."

The waiter brought our entrées, set them down, then motioned behind him."Your meals are compliments of your friend in the corner. He's already paid." He added, "Including tip."

We both turned our heads. "Where is he?"

The waiter looked over in the direction he had motioned. "He's gone, disappeared. He was there a few minutes ago."

Perhaps it was Robert as a thank you for the ballet ticket. "What did he look like?" I asked.

"Late thirties, tall, curly hair. Nice eyes, great body. Anyway, enjoy!"

Margarite raised her eyebrows. "Any ideas on who might have paid for our dinner? I can't think of anyone with that description."

"Had he been older, I might have guessed Robert? I have no idea at all. It must have been someone we know. Could it have been a parent of one of your students?"

"And not stop by. I doubt it. It's kind of exciting, a mystery man."

I smiled. A mystery man. Margarite would find that exciting. It must have been someone she knew. I took a bite of the eggplant Parmigiana. It was excellent.

Margarite put her glass down. "Robert sure seems to want to rekindle your romance."

"He definitely seems to." I started to feel my heart beat in overtime. "Remember, I've been burned by him once."

Margarite grimaced.

"He called this afternoon before I left for ballet class. We're going to the Impressionist Fashion Exhibition tomorrow."

Margarite's eyes lit up. "That's wonderful."

I could feel my face flush. "I need to be careful not to get burned again."

"People do change, mature." Margarite took a bite of her chicken. "I'd like to go to the exhibit also."

"It will be here for a while. I'd be happy to go again. We could go some weekend."

Chapter Five

Tuesday, February 17

When I heard the garbage truck pass, I looked out of the front window and saw Tricia and Alice coming from across the street with bags of groceries. With all of their activities planned, Tricia must have taken a second day off. It was starting to snow lightly.

I opened my front door to leave to meet Robert. Today we were going to the Impressionist Fashion Exhibition which I had been looking forward to for months. Thinking about the snow, I decided to get a warmer cap and a scarf and started searching through my front closet, leaving the door slightly ajar.

Alice's stern voice sounded from the hallway. "Don't tell me you're changing your mind again. Look how he treats you."

I hustled over to the door and closed it just before they reached their door across the hall and put my ear up against it. Alice always seemed to instigate trouble. Stephen and Tricia weren't as close as they had been. I often heard them arguing.

What was Tricia changing her mind about? Was Stephen abusing her and she told me the story about getting bruised at work to cover it up? Was she thinking about going to the police? I still didn't believe that of Stephen.

"Shh. There must be another way," Tricia said.

"Too late for that," Alice said, sounding quite ominous in a voice overpowering Tricia's.

What was that all about? It almost sounded like Alice was talking about revenge. What had they done that it was too late? I looked through the peephole. Perhaps they thought I was gone and couldn't hear them.

Their door closed. When I opened mine, I looked down the hall and saw Robert waving from outside the brownstone.

Locking my door quietly, I tiptoed down the hall, and opened the front door for Robert. "I was going to start walking to meet you," I said in a low voice.

His voice wavered. "Shall we get a taxi? It's snowing."

"Let's walk the few blocks and take the crosstown bus through Central Park."

I closed the front door.

"Why are we whispering by the way?"

As we headed out to the bus, I told Robert about my neighbors and the short bits of conversation I had just heard. "And now Alice and Tricia are arguing."

"Do you think something sinister is going on?" he asked.

"I don't know. I don't have a concrete reason to suspect anything, but why would Alice have said, 'Too late for that?'"

"Confront Tricia. Perhaps Alice is trying to talk her sister into divorcing Stephen or the sister has already started proceedings."

I shrugged. "I hope Tricia isn't, especially with how sick Stephen has been. Robert, do you know Stephen from somewhere? The other day when I introduced the two of you, there seemed to be a spark of recognition."

"On his side?"

"On both your parts."

His lips pressed together. "Must have been your imagination." He then smiled and put his arm through mine. "Irina, I'm really looking forward to the art exhibition."

As we waited for the crosstown bus at 86th Street, I thought about Stephen mentioning he was always taking Tricia's health concoctions. Whatever herbs they were using weren't working. Stephen seemed to be getting worse rather than better. Maybe sometimes the cure was worse than the ailment. But how can you treat with herbs, when you don't actually know what is wrong? Stephen hadn't been to a doctor.

"Irina...the bus. It's here."

While travelling through the park, I watched Robert as he looked out the window. His was a kind face. I said, "I can't think of anything better than enjoying a day in the city."

He turned towards me and smiled. "I haven't been in Central Park since I've been back."

"Let's plan on going into the park after the museum then."

The bus left us off close to the museum. We entered into the soaring Great Hall of The Metropolitan Museum of Art with its immense domes and dramatic lofty arches. Crowds flowed through it. Robert paid our admission, all the while I looked around the ceilings.

I glanced in the direction of the Egyptian Wing. "Over the Christmas holidays I went to a reception for The Manhattan Music Project in the Temple of Dendur. Imagine having dinner in an Egyptian monument built by Emperor Augustus in 15 B.C. It was breathtaking." I suggested that later I take him to The Sackler Wing and would show him the room if he liked. We turned and headed toward the exhibition gallery.

We strolled through the crowded galleries of the Impressionist Fashion in Art Exhibition commenting on the allure of the stylish Parisian's dress when Impressionism came of age. It felt comfortable being on Robert's arm. He had changed since college, having never been particularly interested in art or going to museums. As we progressed

58

through the exhibition, we saw how the artists' took their palettes outdoors, capturing the nature of the ever-changing light and shade with the latest trends in fashion. Towards the end was a Degas painting of The Millinery Shop.

Degas was one of my favorite artists. After we finished the last gallery, Robert reminded me of my promise to go to Temple of Dendur. Soon he became immersed in the Egyptian Art. When I realized he wanted to read every label, every caption of every piece, I excused myself and told him he could meet up with me on the second floor in one of the Degas rooms after he had finished.

There were four Degas rooms at The Met. Perhaps it even held the largest Degas collection of any museum. I'd need to ask Tricia about that. I was especially drawn to his dancer paintings. The rooms were much less crowded than on first floor. I walked past Degas' imposing bronze sculpture, "The Little Fourteen-Year-Old Dancer" into the second room. I believed that if a girl wanted to be a ballerina at a young age, it was partly due to viewing Edgar Degas' ballet paintings. It had been for me, plus with my mother being a ballerina. Slowly moving from one painting to another, I became completely absorbed in his work, observing his depiction of movement in the paintings and his choice of unusual viewpoints, angles at which ballet was never meant to be viewed.

Degas showed the world of the ballet with truthfulness; the ideal versus reality, the beauty, but also the difficulties of achieving perfection.

I sat down on a bench in front of "The Rehearsal of the Ballet Onstage" totally mesmerized. The painting grew more complex with analysis. My eyes moved during a random glance with the fluidity of movement in the painting.

As I focused closer on the painting, I thought I heard the sound of strings. Turning around, I saw only the museum guard standing in the doorway. He glanced at me, then looked away.

I stood up and moved closer to the painting. Degas' technique of using pastels in long, undulating lines over the base coat of oil, gave the painting the same vibrancy and energy of the dancers. I watched as the ballet dancers stretched in rehearsal, then saw the purity of the dance itself, romantic and feminine, their attention to the footwork, the carriage of their arms. Suddenly the layers of tulle netting in one dancer's full skirts blocked the view of another's foot movements.

I stretched my neck to the right to see the details of the blocked dancer's point work, then slowly I inched over to where Degas was painting. The detail of it did not escape his eye. Working quickly, Degas captured the dancer's footwork. I stood behind Degas watching the dancers and watched his depiction of them. After putting the finishing touches on his painting, he turned around and looked up at me.

"Tres belle!" I whispered to him.

He smiled, his eyes bright and spoke but a single, "Merci." With a contented smile, he turned back to his canvas.

An enchanting melody drifted across the rehearsal room. Degas completed his name, then put his brush down. He wiped his fingers on a soft cloth that was attached to his easel, then finished watching the dance. Looking at Degas' profile, I saw a single tear escape from his eye.

"Irina...Irina, there you are."

I heard Robert's voice, lifted up my head, and looked over towards him.

He was all smiles. "I can't believe that you dosed off sitting here on the bench. How late did you stay out with Margarite?"

I glanced around the room. "I must have nodded off just for a few minutes. It's quite warm in here."

"There's a Monet two rooms over I'd like to show you."

Standing up, I hooked my arm through Robert's. As I left the room, I glanced back at "The Rehearsal of the Ballet Onstage" smiled, then blew a kiss.

After finishing the many rooms in the Impressionist Wing, we decided to leave and walked a block along Central Park entering on East 84th Street. The light was starting to cast purple shadows on the snow. The lamps came on. Few people were around where we entered, other than a cross-country skier having difficulty maneuvering and a couple walking by with their dogs. We walked up a slope to find kids sledding down a blue and purple tinged hill, screeching with delight. Following the bends in the path, we stopped to regard a half melted snowman. The remnants of the eyes, nose, and mouth were laying next to the mounds of snow.

"Remember building a snowman here when we were in college?"

I smiled. "Yes. You donated your scarf for the effort."

Robert turned a full circle. "Central Park is no less lovely in the winter. I've missed Manhattan."

I smiled. So you keep saying. "I love the trees naked against the sky." I put my gloved hands into my coat pockets. It was freezing.

He laughed. "The trees aren't the only thing I want to see naked."

I laughed. My cheeks must have turned as pink as the gorgeous sunset. Even though I didn't want to ruin the illusion of Robert only being here because of me, I asked again, "Robert why did you really come to Manhattan?"

Robert put his arm around my shoulder and kissed my cheek. His lips were warm. He looked at me and smiled. Warmth instantly spread down the back of my neck. "You mean beside you being here?" He laughed again. "I'm checking out commercial real estate. I'm interested in investing." He pulled me towards him and kissed my lips.

I smiled. His kisses caught me off-guard, although they shouldn't have. I felt the air charge. "Let's go catch the bus."

* * * *

On the way back, we stopped at Zabar's to pick up a few things for a quick dinner. When we turned the corner to another aisle I could hear Tricia and Alice talking. I was surprised to see them here, since they had been grocery shopping earlier.

"Stephen loves lasagna. He always eats two pieces," Alice said. "We should make it for him when he gets back tomorrow evening."

Maybe Alice was coming around, trying to be more accommodating to Stephen. I was glad to hear it, although it seemed odd that she changed quickly from being almost hateful to caring about him.

They took off walking towards the produce before I had the chance to say anything. "Robert, "Do you see those two women?"

"You mean the ones you were just eavesdropping on?"

"I was not!" I said louder than I expected. A clerk who was re-shelving down the aisle looked in our direction. I smiled at him.

In a lower voice, I said, "I was not eavesdropping. I can't help it if they were talking loudly. That's Alice, Tricia's sister."

"The Alice that you are so suspicious of. She doesn't look that sinister."

I rolled my eyes, then Tricia and Alice turned into the aisle almost bumping into our cart.

"Hello there," I said.

"Hello. We didn't see you," Tricia replied. They looked at Robert.

"Alice, this is Robert, the friend of mine from college. Tricia, you remember Robert from the other day." I had mentioned at Margarite's that he and I were going to The Met today. "Robert, I'd like you to meet Alice."

They shook hands.

"We just came back from The Met. The exhibit was beautiful."

Tricia smiled at us. "Wasn't it fabulous viewing the fashions right next to the paintings they were depicted in?" Tricia said.

"It was extremely well done," I said. "I so enjoyed it."

"We should get going Tricia?" Alice abruptly said and started walking away.

"It was nice seeing you again, Robert," Tricia said, then hastened to catch up with Alice.

Robert raised his eyebrows.

When they were out of earshot, I said, "Well, what do you think?"

"I can see what you're talking about now," he responded.

"Alice is always like that."

After we arrived back at the brownstone, Robert opened a bottle of wine. I turned on the gas fireplace and put on some jazz before going into the kitchen. I readied a platter of three different kinds of salmon, scallion cream cheese, and bagels and placed it on the coffee table in the living room. The rest of the evening we relaxed sitting in the living room with a glass of wine, good conversation, and reminisced about old times.

"Remember, Irina, when we went to the Oscars party and everyone dressed as characters in one of the nominated movies. It was such a fun time." Robert reached for my hand.

"It was a fun party. Actually, it was at Samantha's apartment."

Robert looked thoughtful. "It was my last semester at NYU."

"You went as Rocky Balboa and I as Adrian. It seems I remember you being gone for much of the party and I spent a lot of the evening with Samantha's date."

Robert reached for another bagel sheepishly.

Perhaps I shouldn't have brought up his deceased wife.

"You were a ravishing Adrian."

I laughed.

"Irina, did I tell you, I called an old friend from our NYU days? Do you remember Monica and Todd? I suggested we all get together."

Monica? Finally, we get to Monica. Mysterious Monica. I didn't want to let on that I didn't remember them at all. "I faintly remember them. Are they married?"

"They never took that step. They're anxious to get reacquainted with you. Monica seemed especially interested in your ballet days. We should all go out."

Hmm. Why did Jerome make Monica sound so mysterious? I'll need to ask him about that. "Sure. That would be nice sometime."

"I made a date for us to go out with them Friday evening, at the little Thai restaurant in the Village you mentioned you loved so much."

I raised my eyebrows. "You what? Without consulting me first. What if I was busy?"

He put the bagel down and took a sip of the wine. "Well, we don't have to go, if you'd rather not, I can cancel our plans." He looked up at a painting. "I'm not going to force you."

Our plans? I took a sip of my wine. "It would have been nice to have asked me ahead of making the plans. I'll have to check my calendar." Robert *had* listened about my liking the Thai restaurant.

All was quiet for a few moments while we ate.

Robert glanced at his watch.

I took another sip of wine, then looked at my watch. "It's getting late. I've had a wonderful day, Robert. Thank you."

"It doesn't have to end, you know."

I smiled. "Well, for me it does. I'm exhausted."

Robert got up and helped clear the table. Before leaving he gave me an insistent kiss. "Think about Friday, okay?"

Why the persistence on meeting up with Monica and Todd? "Good night, Robert."

"How about tomorrow evening? I'll come over and make you dinner."

"Sounds like a date."

After Robert left, I thought about it and found it strange he didn't invite me to his place tomorrow evening to make dinner so I could see his new apartment.

Chapter Six

Wednesday, February 18

I was right in the middle of a thrilling part in the mystery *The Ginseng Conspiracy*, when I heard a knock at the door. Reluctantly, I put the book down and opened the door to find Stephen holding a bouquet of flowers.

"You're back from the conference. Stephen, you look great. Tanned." I looked at the gorgeous yellow roses.

He held them out. "These are for you."

I took the bouquet from him. "They're lovely, Stephen. Thank you. What a beautiful color." Smelling the flowers I asked, "What's the occasion?"

"Me being a rude, irrational jerk the other day."

"Nonsense. You weren't at all. Do you have time to come in?"

"Sure, for a little while."

I moved aside while smelling the flowers again. They had a wonderful fragrance. Giving me roses was a bit much, but they were beautiful. "There wasn't any need for flowers, although I do love them. You looked quite sick that day. I knew that was it."

I put the roses on the coffee table. I'd put them in water later. We sat down.

"I was sick, Irina. I've been feeling quite ill lately. I thought I should go to the doctor, but Tricia insisted it was the flu and I'd feel better soon. And she was right. I feel much better. The sun and warmer weather must have been just what I needed."

Quite the opposite of what Tricia had told me when she said Stephen felt whatever he had was passing. "Yes, Florida definitely agreed with you. I'm so happy that you're feeling well. I bet Tricia is glad you're back."

His smile wavered. "I haven't seen Tricia or Alice yet. Perhaps being away from them agrees with me also." He laughed a nervous laugh.

"Troubles?"

Stephen shook his head. "Tricia says I'm not being considerate of her, I'm too self-centered. That I don't listen. I know this is all Alice's doings. She's putting ideas into Tricia's head about me."

A blood vessel started twitching in his left temple area.

"Tricia and I seem to argue all of the time. I can hardly say a word to Alice and she'll jump on me about something. I shouldn't have to live like this in my own home."

"I'm so sorry, Stephen." I reached for his hand and lightly squeezed it.

"I can't take it any longer, Irina. I talked to Tricia before I left for the conference. Alice must move out. She has to get her own place."

"How did Tricia respond to that?"

"Tricia argues that Manhattan is too expensive."

"Well, it is expensive. Perhaps Alice could move in with a friend."

"She's been here for almost six months and hasn't made any friends...at all. She doesn't seem to like anyone in her writing group."

I didn't find that hard to believe. Alice had an abrasive personality.

67

"Tricia is her social life."

I didn't know how to respond.

He scratched his neck. "Recently I've talked to a lawyer about—"

A door slammed in the hallway. "Oh, no, Stephen, a lawyer?"

Stephen looked over towards the door. His face reddened. "That's probably them now. Tricia has to make a decision. Is it going to be Alice or me?"

"I'm sorry everything has gotten that bad and has come to this."

"I better get going. Unfortunately, my racquetball partner Alex texted. He reserved the court for tonight."

"The man that drove you to the airport?"

Stephen stood up and started for the door. "Right. I'll be lucky to get dinner in before I have to leave." He glanced at his watch.

I hoped he had time for dinner, Tricia and Alice were making lasagna especially for him this evening. "Couldn't you cancel?"

Stephen shook his head. "He's so persistent about playing. He wants to do drills and start playing doubles. He doesn't know, but I plan to get a new partner soon. I've had it with his cheating. He's the type of guy that will do anything to win. He's the same way in the workplace."

Stephen must have thought I had a questioning look, which I did, because why would he play with a cheater?

Stephen's eyebrows drew together. He reached for the door knob. "If he can't make a shot, he calls a hinder. Many of his other calls are absurd."

I wrinkled my brow. I had no idea about the rules of racquetball and why Stephen would play with a cheater.

"*I know*. Saying all of that, other times he's generous. For instance, taking me to the airport a few days ago. And he does other favors. Plus he's an office-mate. I've tried to remain civil and be a team player, but things are going to change real soon. *For everything!*"

Stephen opened the door.

"One quick question. When I introduced you to Robert the other evening it almost seemed like you had met each other previously."

"We had past dealings at the agency. Somewhat negative."

"What do you mean, negative?"

I heard someone coming into the front door stamping their feet.

"Another time. I better get going. Have a great evening, Irina."

"Thank you, and thanks again for the lovely flowers. I'm glad to see you are doing well, Stephen. I was quite worried about you. I'm relieved you look so much better."

He turned around and smiled. "You're welcome. Thanks for listening. And don't worry about me, I'll be fine. Changes are on their way." He left.

I closed the door. "Now to get the flowers in water," I said aloud. Thinking about what Stephen had just said, I took the roses into the kitchen and got down a vase from an upper cupboard. Those changes were going to be tough ones. How was Tricia going to deal with the ultimatum? How was Alice going to deal with it? Should I talk to Tricia? We were close at one time.

The physical change in Stephen was as different as night and day, from knocking on death's door to what I had just seen, a picture of health. Well, perhaps he wasn't as bad as I thought he was before or had he been? How could you get better in just a few days?

After cutting off the bottom of each stem, I arranged the flowers in the glass vase and smelled them again on the way back into the living room. I set the vase down on the table by the front window.

Glancing out the front window, I saw the man approaching my building I had seen so often previously. I grabbed my coat out of the front closet and ran to the outer door and hastened down the stairs, my hands sliding along the concrete balustrade. I slipped on the last icy step and fell. "Wait!" I called out to him.

The man, already a couple buildings down turned around, and hurried back to me. "Are you all right? Let me help you up."

When I got back on my feet, I asked, "Who are you?"

He smiled. A very nice smile. Again, I thought he looked strangely familiar.

"Pardon me?"

I laughed. "You look familiar. Do I know you? I've seen you around quite often lately walking past my home, my ballet studio, when I look out of restaurant windows." I knew I sounded crazy, but he seemed to be everywhere. Also I was starting to make him sound like a stalker.

He also laughed. "I'm new to the neighborhood, to Manhattan actually, and I enjoy walking. My name is Michel, Michel Dupont."

"French?"

His smile was warm. "Oui, Madame. My name is French."

I smiled. His face was gentle. I didn't know this man, but I already liked him. I held out my hand. "I'm Irina. Welcome to the neighborhood. How do you like living here so far?"

"I love the Upper West Side. Manhattan is amazing. It's so alive."

"That it is. What do you do here?" Too direct I wondered?

Smiling, his eyes bright, Michel said, "I'm an adjunct professor at Columbia University in the Department of Music."

"I have a friend, who is also a professor in the department."

His eyes fixed on mine, he continued. "I teach composition and music theory. I started this January."

My calf was starting to bother me. I reached down and rubbed it. "How interesting." I put my hand on the railing. I felt I should go back to my apartment and elevate my leg.

I smiled. "It's been lovely meeting you. I'm sure I'll see you again." I knew I would. He seemed to be everywhere. "And the next time, I'll be able to greet you by name." I turned to go up the stairs.

He put his hand on my arm. "Do you need help? You appear to be limping un petit peu."

I smiled. "Thank you, Michel. I'll be okay."

"Would you like to go out for a coffee sometime?"

My eyes widened, then I turned around. "Coffee?" I hesitated for a few seconds. "Yes, I'd like that very much."

Michel smiled. "You could tell me about your ballet studio and the restaurants where you have seen me through the windows."

I laughed. "Do you have a pen and paper?"

He took out his cell phone, put in my number, then we said our goodbyes.

When I entered the building, I could already smell cooking. Tricia must be preparing Stephen's "Welcome Home" dinner. Then I thought about my surprise meal with Robert this evening. What was on the menu?

* * * *

Around six o'clock the doorbell rang. I opened the door to my apartment and saw Robert holding a bag of groceries in each arm. I went and opened the front door.

Robert smiled. "Irina...help!"

I took one of the bags and gave him a peck on his cheek. He gave me a bear hug with his free arm. "I'm so happy to see you. I've been thinking of you all day and missed you. I hope you like the special meal I have planned."

"I can't wait. What are we having?"

71

We walked back into my apartment.

Robert's eyes lit up. "When was the last time you had goulash?"

I hesitated. "I don't think I've ever had goulash."

"Irina, of course you've had goulash. We made it often when we lived together. Lots of times it was all we could afford."

I shook my head. My brows pulling in. "My mind's still a blank."

"The dish we made with ground beef, onions, carrots, mushrooms and tomatoes."

Smiling, I said, "You mean the casserole with the elbow macaroni."

Robert's eyes sparkled. "Yes! The very one."

My eyes opened wide. "And that's what we're having...this evening?"

He laughed. "I thought it would bring back fond memories."

I smiled. "That it will. You're sweet thinking about that."

"Of course I have great bread and a couple bottles of choice wine to go with it. Also everything for a salad."

I gave him another peck on the cheek. Then we put the groceries into the kitchen and I took his coat.

Returning into the room, I said, "Okay, I'm in. What can I do to help?"

Robert put his arms around me and gave me a warm kiss on my lips. Then he took a bottle of wine out of the bag, uncorked it, and poured us each a glass and held a glass out to me. "Let's have a toast first. To a wonderful evening of cooking...your favorite goulash recipe."

I laughed.

He continued. "And to the old days, to rekindling our friendship and more."

I raised my eyebrows. He took a sip and so did I.

We started getting the meal together. It was *a bit* more upscale than what we "used to make." Robert cooked the pancetta in the Dutch oven, then cut and browned the cubed rib eye steak in oil. I started prepping the vegetables, chopping carrots, celery, porcini mushrooms and mincing the garlic and rosemary. It felt like when we were in college cooking together. Robert added a cup of wine, I the tomatoes. Then, he returned the meat and pancetta back into the Dutch oven. After we brought the mixture to a boil, we put it in the oven for an hour.

We went into the living room and sat down on the sofa. I had put a Billie Holiday record on. Robert brought the bottle of wine in the room and poured himself another glass of wine.

"These past few days have been great, Irina. I've enjoyed being with you. You're still the vibrant woman I knew so long ago. You take my breath away."

He always came on a bit too strong. "They have been fun."

Robert looked around the room his eyes settling on the flowers. "Beautiful roses. I hope not from a secret admirer?"

"They're from my neighbor, Stephen."

"Ah, Tricia's husband." Robert looked up at the ceiling, then around the room.

"Robert, do you know Stephen from somewhere?"

"You already asked me that. I never met him before the other day when you introduced us."

"Funny, Stephen said he had met you."

"He must be mistaken. Confusing me with someone else." He looked up at the ceiling again. "I'm glad that you've kept many of the original details in your parents' home when you remodeled it."

"Thank you. What's your apartment like? I'd love to see it. Did you sign a lease or are you on a month to month rent basis?" I took another sip of my wine. "How long do you plan on staying in Manhattan?"

"Perhaps forever." Robert put his arm around my shoulder. "That kind of depends on you. Will you ever let me be part of your life again, Irina? Like we were back in the day?"

"Like we were back in the day? I was hurt when you left abruptly after graduation." As if our four years together meant nothing. "And then no word from you at all, until now."

Robert looked hurt. "There were extenuating circumstances."

"Really?"

The timer went off, I stood up and started for the kitchen. "Such as?"

Robert followed me. "I promise it won't happen again. Please take a chance on me."

He didn't answer what the extenuating circumstances were and I wasn't going to drill him if he wasn't going to be forthcoming. That was in the past. Perhaps I should just enjoy myself and live in the moment. I had needs. So then, why the need to be careful? Because Irina you were burned, a voice said inside my head.

When we reached the kitchen, Robert put on oven mitts and took the pot out of the oven and I added the pearl onions.

Robert's cell phone rang. I could hear a woman's husky voice. He took the call in the other room. I set the timer for another hour for the stew to finish. Glancing in the dining room I saw Robert write on a piece of paper. I went back in the kitchen to give Robert his privacy and took the plates that we would use for dinner, out of the cupboard.

After Robert ended the call, he came back into the kitchen and took out a second bottle of wine.

"Sorry about that. Um, that was about a building I'm going to look at tomorrow. Honestly, nothing that couldn't have waited until morning. I don't even know why they had to phone this evening."

Nervously, he took his reading glasses out of his jacket pocket to read the bottle. Numerous papers fell to the ground. He quickly picked up the papers, then uncorked the wine to let it breathe before dinner.

Did he always get this edgy about business?

Robert helped finish setting the dining room table. When I put Stephen's flowers in the center of the table I thought about him and hoped he enjoyed his dinner with Tricia and Alice and was able to cancel on racquetball.

Close to nine o'clock we finally sat down to eat. I was starving, only having had a couple of pieces of Robert's excellent bread when I cut it.

"This is absolutely delicious, Robert."

Robert smiled and raised his glass again. "Just like it was forty years ago. A toast to the cooks."

I smiled as we clinked glasses. I never had goulash like this.

We chatted comfortably over dinner talking about mutual friends, significant events that happened over the years, our current interests. It almost felt as if forty years hadn't passed.

Around eleven o'clock Robert hinted he stay over. I ignored his hint. We ended up making plans to have pizza soon and watch a movie. Again, here. He didn't offer to do so in his apartment.

I watched out the window as he went down the stairs of the brownstone. He looked up at my window. I waved. He smiled and walked out of view.

When I went into the kitchen to turn the lights off, I noticed a paper peeking out from under the island. I picked it up. Robert must have missed this one. Monica's name was on it and a date written. And it wasn't for Friday.

I'd keep that date for Friday. As Jerome had said, I needed to find out about Monica.

Chapter Seven

Thursday, February 19

I was coming back from taking down the garbage, when I saw Stephen staggering in the hallway leaving for work. He almost appeared drunk. My mouth fell open. "Stephen, what happened, you looked so well yesterday?"

"I don't know, Irina. I felt fine after dinner and even played racquetball." Stephen wiped drool from his mouth. "I feel like *crap* this morning. Sorry. I have this *huge* headache and feel nauseous."

The smell of baking permeated from my apartment. I closed the door that I had left ajar. "You sound out of breath as well. You shouldn't be going to work."

"I have to go in to the office today. I'm working on a big project that will determine whether I get promoted to an advertising executive position."

I swallowed hard. I had a terrible apprehensive feeling about him. "You need to see a doctor."

He wiped his mouth again with his hand and attempted a deep breath. "When I have time. Later. Maybe tomorrow. I do *need* to talk to you after work. About Tricia and Alice. Something's not right."

I jumped on his statement. "What? What's not right?"

He looked at his watch then headed toward the door, mumbling, "No time now. I'm going to be late."

"I'll be here all afternoon until early evening. I have a fundraiser to go to after that," I called after him as he went out the door. I hoped he would make it to the office.

Should I approach Tricia again about Stephen's condition? I had failed to get any results the first two times. How could she have let him leave home in his condition? She must have seen how Stephen looked. She didn't start work until later in the morning.

And what was so important that he *needed* to talk to me after work? He had already hinted at a divorce yesterday. Had Tricia responded negatively to his ultimatum regarding Alice?

Knowing Margarite had taken the day off to get ready for the fundraiser this evening, I knocked on her door and invited her over for a quick cup of coffee. She could probably use the break. She said she'd be right over.

While I waited, I put on a Diana Krall album and set the table. I took Mascarpone cheese and homemade lemon curd, that I had made for the currant scones, out of the refrigerator. As I put Stephen's flowers on the table, the doorbell rang.

"I'm so glad you could make it, Margarite. I know you have a lot on your mind."

"This evening will be fabulous. I'm so excited. I have a few last minute details to see to this morning, but thanks for the invite."

Margarite headed a group of business people, educators, artists, and others who were interested in "social justice", making a difference for a kinder, fairer world. This evening was an important fundraiser for the different causes. I belonged and was involved with a women and children's shelter, SAFE, Inc. I wanted to be a positive contributor to the community. Last week I worked on writing grants for housing, education, and child care.

She leaned in. "So what's on your mind?"

Margarite knew me well. "Stephen. I can't get Stephen off of my mind. What can we do about him?" We went into the kitchen and sat down at the table in front of my sunny yellow window.

"I don't see that we can do anything." Margarite leaned over to smell the flowers. "Beautiful roses. Yellow? From Robert?"

"No, they're from Stephen. I'm worried about Stephen."

"He's still sick?"

I poured Margarite a cup of coffee. "Help yourself to the scones. Did you by chance see him yesterday?"

"No."

"I have this horrible feeling." I told Margarite about how well Stephen looked after he came home from his trip and how he looked this morning. "Something is terribly wrong. Even Stephen knows that. He's coming over after work to talk."

Margarite added milk and sugar to her coffee and reached for a scone. "I'm glad he feels that comfortable with you."

"As soon as Tricia and Stephen moved in I felt close to them. We did many activities together, eating out, movies. You were with us a couple of times. We enjoyed each other's company, right? With Alice, the opposite. Everything...life annoys her."

"Stephen is probably feeling the physical effects of negative energy around him," Margarite said.

My eyes opened wide. "Negative energy. I never thought of that. And being away gave him the ability to recharge." I spread a thin layer of Mascarpone cheese on my scone and topped it with a dab of lemon curd. I took a bite. Delicious, but no time for mindfulness.

"Sure, the stress of dealing with negative people often shows up as physical symptoms. It happens all the time with the kids I teach. Being sick and not attending school. Do you believe for a moment Stephen had given Tricia those bruises on her arms?"

"Not at all. It's not in Stephen and Tricia denies any wrong doing. I don't know how I ever could have thought he did. They're just not the same loving couple they were when they moved in. Some kind of intervention is warranted."

Margarite took a sip of her tea. "Their problem is Alice."

"Of course it is. She has a streak of ugliness in her. But what can we do about her?"

Margarite shrugged her shoulders. "I don't see that we can do anything."

I was at a loss about what we could do also. It was heartbreaking to see someone slipping away, right in front of my eyes. I had spoken to both Stephen and Tricia. Why weren't they seeing a major problem that was so evident?

"Sometimes people need to work things out for themselves. What's going on with you and Robert?"

I smiled, needing to think of something else. "He wanted to stay the night."

She hesitated then said, "And you said...?"

"I told him no."

Margarite raised her eyebrows and smiled. "Oh, I see."

"What do you see?"

"Nothing." She took a sip of her coffee, smiling. "Are you happy when you're with Robert? Excited to see him?"

"I suppose I am."

"Just suppose?"

"Okay, I am. I just want to be cautious. Somehow I can't envision a future with Robert. He seems secretive."

"Tall, dark, handsome and mysterious. And you're having problems with that? Might he being playing at being mysterious to entice you."

I rolled my eyes. "I doubt that."

Margarite smiled and nodded her head, then took a bite of her scone. "What time will you arrive at the fundraiser this evening?"

"Robert's coming around seven o'clock."

"I'm going to get there by six to make sure their caterer and everything is set up. I hope we bring in the necessary money for our programs. We have the art gallery until ten o'clock.

"Soho Gallery Paule was a great choice. It's up and coming," I said.

"We were lucky to get on their calendar. It is the perfect venue for our small non-profit. I should get going."

Before she left, I told Margarite about my new friend, Michel. She seemed interested. Her comment, "So many possibilities, Irina."

* * * *

Late that afternoon while going through my closet, trying on different dresses for this evening, all the while keeping an ear out for Stephen coming back home, the phone rang.

"Irina?"

"Yes."

"This is Michel. Remember me, the person you see walking past the windows at restaurants," he said in a humorous tone.

I knew I would never live that down. "Hello Michel. Yes, of course I remember you."

"Would you like to have coffee tomorrow afternoon?"

I moved aside a couple of dresses and sat on the edge of my bed. "Tomorrow afternoon, I teach ballet. I could afterwards. Would you like to meet me at my studio? It's Little Cygnet's Ballet Academy on 84th and—"

He laughed. "I know where it is."

My eyes widened. Yes, you do.

"What time would be convenient?" Michel asked.

"Four o'clock."

"That will be great. Thank you. See you then."

Smiling, I hung up the phone. I went into the living room to retrieve my purse that I had left on the sofa, when I heard a door slam in the hallway. I looked out the peephole and didn't see anyone, but I could hear angry, raised voices. I could hear Stephen's voice, but I couldn't tell if the other voice was Tricia's or Alice's. Not wanting to interfere, but still wanting to know what was going on, I went out and checked my mailbox, lingering in the hallway for a while. When I came back to my apartment, things had quieted down. Had Stephen forgotten he planned to come over?

By the time Robert arrived, Stephen still hadn't come over. Perhaps he had forgotten, although I doubted that.

"Your dress. It's quite the show stopper!" Robert said as he helped me with my coat. I had decided on a knee-length classic black and white, graphic patterned dress. It had a sleek silhouette.

"Thank you." I complimented him on his artsy vest.

A taxi was waiting. We headed downtown. I looked out the window, watching the night life as we drove down Broadway, past the sensory overload of Times Square and the people pouring into the Theatre District, all the while thinking about Stephen. Why hadn't he come over?

"Earth to Irina. I just asked you what you thought about..."

"I'm sorry. I keep thinking about my neighbor Stephen across the hall. Remember, I told you about Stephen and Tricia and Alice and about how something wasn't quite right? Things have gotten even worse."

"They could be headed for a divorce. Over fifty percent of all marriages—"

"And with a sister-in-law like Alice, make that seventy-five percent. She's getting in the way of their marriage. Stephen and Tricia both need to put their foot down if there is any hope left. Tricia says Alice can't afford Manhattan on her own.

"If rents are too high in Manhattan, she can move to Brooklyn."

I sighed heavily. "Brooklyn isn't exactly affordable either, especially for a struggling writer. In fact, the price gap is closing between Manhattan and Brooklyn. Brooklyn is way on the rise."

Robert looked ahead. "It's best not to worry about things you have no control over."

My mind went back to thinking about them. Stephen and Tricia had a communication breakdown. Robert was right, I couldn't do anything about it, other than being available to lend a sympathetic ear to either of them. But I think their problem went way beyond communication. It was much worse than that.

I told Robert about meeting my new acquaintance for coffee the next day. "You know how people say they knew someone in another life. It feels like that. He's so familiar."

"Our date with Monica and Todd is tomorrow."

I slightly shook my head. "This is hours before. Don't worry, nothing will interfere with Monica and Todd," I said with a tinge of sarcasm in my voice that went over Robert's head.

"I can come with you if you'd like. You don't know who this guy is?"

"Not necessary. Michel seems like a very nice man—"

"Those can be the worst."

I frowned, looked out the window, then turned back to Robert. "It's in the middle of the afternoon. And I've lived in Manhattan all of my life. I can take care of myself."

Robert didn't respond and looked ahead again.

We arrived at the Soho Gallery Paule on Mercer Street. Entering through a black painted doorway, we were warmly welcomed by one of the educators Margarite taught with. I glanced around looking for Margarite. A large crowd already had gathered. I met up with several friends and introduced Robert. While mingling, I noticed how easily Robert fit in with everyone and seemed to enjoy himself. It was great being here with him.

A trio was playing: a saxophonist, bass player and percussion. A few of the women were out on the floor in front of the trio, teetering on their heels. Margarite came over dressed as dazzling as the energy in the gallery. She greeted Robert and me and said, "Isn't this great? What a turnout!"

"I'm so happy. It's the high-energy scene you hoped for." I smiled. "You definitely chose the right venue."

"You helped me."

"Oh, that's right, I did." I laughed.

"The staff went out of their way to accommodate us. Have you tasted the food yet? Fabulous caterers. Everything is running smoothly. I see someone with deep pockets I need to speak with. Catch you later." She turned around and looked at Robert before leaving. "Great vest, by the way!"

"Second compliment of the evening," he said smiling.

A waiter in a white Nehru jacket and black pants wandered by and offered us a variety of hors d'oeuvres from his tray. I chose a chili rock shrimp, Robert a smoked salmon canape. After Robert finished the canape, he went to get drinks. I was surprised to see Tricia and Alice coming towards me. Alice looked quite on-trend in a black jumpsuit with a striking waistband of shades of teal and magenta. Tricia wore more of a party dress, a printed taffeta mini-dress number.

"You made it this evening." I was wondering how they could come when Stephen looked so ill again.

"We won't be able to stay long. Stephen's not feeling well," Tricia said.

"I'm sorry to hear that."

"I love this gallery." Tricia quickly changed the subject.

"It's one of our favorites when gallery-hopping," Alice said.

Tricia looked around the walls at the art work. "So intimate."

This gallery was quite large. There were a number of rooms in the building, including a roof loft. I smiled. "You're used to fundraisers at The Met," I said.

Robert joined us, handing me a glass of red wine. I took a sip of the wine. Full-bodied. Not the usual inexpensive wine many art galleries were known for. He visited with Tricia and Alice a couple of minutes before he asked, "What can I get you ladies at the bar?"

After Robert left, Alice smiled again and said, "We were just to a fundraiser at The Met."

I was happy to see that Alice was enjoying herself. "It must have been quite the event." I looked around. "I hope we do well here this evening."

Another waiter came over and this time I chose a maple-glazed scallop. Tricia and Alice each chose a pesto-grilled shrimp.

"Alice volunteers at Little Sisters, Inc.," Tricia said. "They had a fundraiser last month."

Really? "How fabulous, Alice. I didn't know that. Little Sisters is a great program."

Alice beamed. "I've been working behind the scenes, but next month I'm going to be a mentor to a twelve-year-old sister. I wanted to take on a more personal role."

I hoped they did psychological profiles on their big sisters. "Interesting."

Robert returned, handing them their drinks.

"Think of the young life Alice will change," Tricia said.

I was thinking about just that when the music stopped. Margarite went up to the podium, welcomed everyone, and spoke with poise and great enthusiasm about the various programs we were supporting. She didn't speak long, just over ten minutes. She asked everyone to dig deep into their pockets for these great causes. When she finished, everyone clapped. I was proud of Margarite and grateful to be part of this group, pushing our programs forward to have the most impact, trying to make the world a better place.

The music started up again. Robert and I left to look at the art work. This gallery was more cutting-edge, belonging to the avant-garde of New York's art scene. Clusters of paintings were arranged on the walls by theme. I turned back. Tricia and Alice had joined a group of others closer to their ages.

"Alice isn't quite what I expected after Zabar's," Robert said.

"Believe me. She was on her best behavior." I told Robert about her volunteering at Little Sisters. "I hope she does well by the child."

"She may have a redeeming value after all, Irina."

I smiled. We stopped in front of a painting. "This has a Warholesque aura."

Robert smiled. "You're right, Irina. Can't say I like it, but totally Andy Warhol."

Margarite came over and said quietly, "Irina, we are doing well. Very well. Everything is going full force with more people still arriving. And none leaving."

"I'm glad to hear it."

"You would have loved it. A few people are making public displays when giving, I'll tell you about them later, but who cares. As long as we raise the much needed funds."

"That's what's important," I said.

"I couldn't have done this, Irina, without your help planning the event. And thank you, Robert for your generous contribution."

I looked over at Robert, pleased. He must have made a contribution when getting our drinks.

"I better get back. Keep your fingers crossed."

Around nine-thirty we left. I hadn't seen Tricia and Alice for over a half hour.

When we reached my apartment, Robert kissed me gently on my neck. "Irina, I had a wonderful evening. I'm so happy when I'm with you. I think we need to spend more time together. I can stay the night. We can just stay up and talk."

"I teach ballet tomorrow." I was glad that my leg was feeling better. I smiled thinking about running to meet up with Michel and slipping on the steps. Suddenly I realized my smile might be sending an affirmative message to Robert.

"I'll leave right after breakfast. You'll have plenty of time. I really think this is important."

I didn't say anything.

He walked me to my apartment and waited until I had unlocked the door and turned on the living room light.

"I've had another wonderful evening with you," he said matter-of-factly. "I'll call you tomorrow with the time for our dinner with Monica and Todd."

I smiled. "Good night, Robert. I had a great time also."

He kissed me again, this time on my cheek.

After Robert left, I went to the window and watched him walk down the stairs outside like I did yesterday. Again he looked up at my window and paused. I put my hand up to the glass and smiled. He smiled, reached in his pocket and went over to the taxi, then turned around and ran up the stairs taking two at a time. I met him at the outside door. We embraced and walked back to my apartment.

Chapter Eight

After midnight, I woke to the wail of sirens getting louder and louder, closer and closer. Like a shot, I jumped out of bed. Robert wasn't in the room. Putting on my robe, I went into the living room where I found him looking out the window.

"Robert, what's going on?"

He turned around. "I don't know. Whatever it is, it's something big."

I looked out the window to see an ambulance and police cars with flashing lights in front of our building. There was a commotion in the hallway. I opened the door. Police officers along with EMS personnel were filing into Tricia and Stephen's apartment. My heart raced. I hoped it wasn't Stephen.

Margarite stood at her door as well, watching the activity. She came over to me. "I wonder what's going on?"

A chill went down my spine. I had a bad feeling. I couldn't get any words out regarding what I suspected was going on.

Curiosity got the better of us. After the hallway was once again empty we walked over to Tricia and Stephen's apartment door and looked in. Alice was sitting on the sofa in the living room looking toward the shaded windows. We followed the sound of voices into the kitchen. Tricia was crying, talking to the police. Down the hallway there were more voices coming from the bedrooms.

The first thing I noticed after seeing Tricia and the policewoman was that their kitchen was spotless. Normally it was quite cluttered with bowls of herbs covering the counters. While Tricia stood with the officer I went close to the dishwasher and opened it slightly. Empty. Often there were dishes in the sink. Everything was immaculate. Immediately I had this strong feeling something was off.

I felt a touch on my shoulder and turned around. It was Robert. "Irina, it's best if we go back and leave everyone to their jobs."

I needed to find out where Stephen was. Why he was missing from the scene? Obviously he must have been in the bedroom. I gave a dismissive wave. "You can go back. I'll be there in a bit."

Margarite looked between Robert and me, raised her eyebrows and gave me a half-smile. Then turned back towards Tricia who was now sobbing.

Margarite came over after Robert left and whispered, "Robert stayed over?"

"Not now," I said with a grave expression watching Tricia.

Margarite looked down the hallway toward the bedrooms. "Where's Stephen?"

"He must still be in the bedroom." I continued to hear voices coming from the bedrooms. "What's taking so long in there?"

I noticed Robert lingering in the doorway of the living room talking to one of the EMS personnel. What was he still doing here?

"Looks like Robert is getting the scoop on what's going on," Margarite whispered.

"More than what we're finding out."

When Tricia was finished speaking with the police officer, I immediately went over to her. "What's happened? Is Stephen okay?"

She started in crying again. "Stephen's dead."

I let out a gasp. My entire body tensed. "What? Stephen?" I could hear my heart pounding.

"Stephen's dead," Margarite repeated.

I suddenly felt terribly ill. A wave of nausea rose from my stomach. A few moments later, guilt set in. I should have done something, anything. I should have insisted Stephen get to a doctor instead of just suggesting it, when he was looking so poorly. If only he had gone to the doctor.

"After we came back from the fundraiser, he had already gone to bed. Remember I told you he wasn't feeling well. Alice and I watched a movie. Later I heard noises coming from the bedroom. I thought he had gotten up for a drink of water. By the time I came to bed after eleven-thirty, he was already cold. I went into Alice's room and we called 9-1-1. I don't know what happened to him."

Could a person even get cold that fast? "What a terrible shock."

"Excuse me," a police officer said to Margarite and me, "You'll both have to leave."

Tricia said to the officer, "It's okay. They're friends."

When the police officer left the room, Margarite put her arms around Tricia. "I'm so sorry."

Tricia wiped her eyes. "How will I ever go on without him? He was my whole life."

We led Tricia into the living room, thinking she should sit down before she fell over. Alice stood in front of her plants by the window. It might have been my imagination, but it looked like she was glaring at me? Why would she be, at a time like this? Margarite walked over to her, while Tricia and I sat on the sofa, Tricia sobbing again. I reached for her hand. Mine was trembling. Her's were cold.

Margarite glanced at me, then asked Alice, "What happened here tonight?"

"After we got back from the fundraiser, Stephen had already gone to bed. We had mentioned to Irina at the fundraiser he wasn't feeling well. Tricia and I watched a movie and then Tricia went to bed about eleven thirty. Stephen wasn't breathing. We called 9-1-1 immediately."

Alice said almost the exact same thing as Tricia did word for word. And was this the reason they came over and spoke with Robert and I at the gallery, to mention about Stephen?

"He had been declining," Alice added. "Some kind of flu. He had been ill for weeks as you know."

Not when he came back to town from his trip. Just a week ago Tricia and Alice denied Stephen being sick. I wanted to scream, "Liar!" I took my hand away from Tricia's. I didn't need to be a psychic to know something wasn't right here. I was getting a bad vibe, that was on the verge of sinister, from both of the sisters.

Tricia got up from the sofa. I heard her say to another police officer when he came into the living room, "He had been declining for the past few weeks. He was so sick, some kind of flu, but he refused to go to the doctor."

I looked between Tricia, Alice, and Margarite. There was an echo in the room. Their stories were so alike, they sounded well-rehearsed.

With the police officer in the room, Alice came over to Tricia and said, "You poor dear. Poor Stephen. I'm so sorry."

Margarite and I looked at each other at the same time, then I slowly shook my head. Really? Poor Stephen? I didn't buy Alice's little display of grief. I'd had enough. I fell silent and took a couple of deep breaths.

A dark feeling continued to settle in. Lots of questions ran through my mind. Margarite and I left and went out in the hallway.

A woman carrying a large camera came in the front door with two other people, perhaps someone from forensics, followed by a man carrying a medical bag. Stopping him I asked, "Are you the coroner?"

He looked at me. "Yes. Are you the wife of the deceased?"

Margarite answered. "Neighbors."

"We think you should consider ordering an autopsy," I said. "Something's not right here."

Before I had a chance to say anymore, he said, "If you'll pardon me, please."

He walked into Tricia's apartment.

By the time I went back to my apartment, Robert had already gone back to bed. Deciding to make a cup of tea to calm my nerves, I went into the kitchen and reached for the tea canister which I kept next to the small basket that held Tricia and Stephen's apartment key. They had given me their key in case of an emergency. The basket had been moved. Robert must have felt the need for tea also before he went back to bed. I moved the basket back to where it belonged.

Chapter Nine

Sleep never came to me the rest of the night. I couldn't quiet my mind. I tossed and turned thinking about my suspicions, something didn't seem right. Tricia and Alice's comments sounded rehearsed. The kitchen was too clean. Where were the herbs that always were on their counters? Why had Stephen looked so well after being away?

Had Tricia really made health concoctions? Or had she put something harmful instead into Stephen's drinks. But she wouldn't do that. Or would she? It seemed more like something Alice might do. Oh my gosh, I remembered when reading in one of Alice's disturbing mysteries, the murder weapon was poison. Would the police be astute and not be fooled by their deception, the story of Stephen being ill?

That morning Robert stayed only long enough for a couple of cups of coffee and a short talk about the events of yesterday evening. I had offered Robert tea; he said he never touched the stuff. After Robert left, I showered and baked muffins to take to Tricia. I was anxious to learn more about what was going on. Poor Stephen. I still couldn't believe he was dead.

Around ten o'clock I knocked on their door. Alice answered in her usual sweet manner. "Oh, you. What do you want?" Perhaps she was manic depressive, being so pleasant at the fundraiser.

Tricia came over to the door still in her robe. "Please come in, Irina."

The living room was dark. Handing her the plate of muffins, I said, "Oh Tricia, I'm so sorry."

I felt Alice's eye on me. Alice opened one of the shades by the front windows letting the light in. I looked over at her when she lifted the second shade and noticed a couple of the herbal plants missing from that sill. She followed my eyes and also looked down at where the plants had been.

"What kind of muffins are they?" Alice asked.

Tricia took the plate from me and said, "Irina, would you like to join us for a cup of coffee?"

"I'm sure Irina has other things to do."

If the "Little Sisters" organization checked out the mentors' neighbors for recommendations, they definitely wouldn't be getting one from me for Alice. "Thank you, Tricia. I'd love to." I followed Tricia into the kitchen. It wasn't as spotless as when the police had been there. Breakfast dishes were in the sink and herbs back on the counter.

Tricia poured us both a cup of coffee. "The police and everyone finally left around three o'clock." She started to tear up again.

I placed the coffee on the table and put my arms around her and repeated my condolences, "I'm so sorry, Tricia."

"I wish he had gone to the doctor. I begged him to go."

"He could be so stubborn. He wouldn't listen," Alice added coming into the room sitting down at the counter on a bar stool. Then she shrugged.

Again the complete opposite of what Stephen had said. I didn't like this at all. Again, something wasn't right here. How many times had I thought just this?

"Hopefully the coroner will do an autopsy to learn the cause of death," I said.

Alice slammed her cup hard on the counter.

I jerked. What a reaction! I was surprised the cup didn't break.

"Why would they?" she asked, her eyes protruding.

A suspicious death. "A healthy young man dies suddenly. That might even be the law."

"Healthy?" Alice said. "He wasn't all that healthy. He had a family history of heart problems. *My God.*"

Tricia started crying again. "I'm sorry, but I don't want anyone mutilating Stephen."

"No, Irina should be sorry. Bringing all of this up, now! Thank you for the muffins, but I think you should leave. You can see how upset you're making Tricia."

When I got to the kitchen doorway, I glanced back at Tricia. She was looking over at Alice, then when she noticed me looking at her, she looked down again.

"Tricia, if I can help out in any way, please call me."

"Thank you," she responded, her head still down.

On my way back to the apartment, I decided to call my friend, Police Lieutenant Charles Whitney about my suspicions. There were too many conflicting conversations. Perhaps the police had suspicions also and an autopsy was already underway.

At first Charles indicated a polite interest in what I had to say. After I told Charles everything I knew, I realized it didn't sound like much, even to me. I still asked, "Stephen was my friend. I owe it to him to see if foul play was involved. Can you find out if an autopsy was ordered?"

"Irina, I'm sorry about your friend. The Senior Medical Examiner will review the case to determine whether an autopsy will be performed. In New York State, the examiner must think one is warranted. If there's anything suspicious, one will be done. Remember, Irina, a death occurred, not a murder."

"Could you please find out, to put my mind at ease?

He hesitated. "I'll see what I can do."

"Thanks, Charles. I'd appreciate that."

He cleared his throat. "So, that was the infamous Robert at the ballet? Are you and he becoming an item again?"

"I don't know. I suppose you could say that."

"Be careful, Irina. I wouldn't want Robert to break your heart again."

"Thank you. I'll keep that in mind."

"Please do. I care about you. Why do you suppose he suddenly came back into your life after all these years?"

Shaking my head, I laughed nervously. "To renew our friendship." And more. "His wife died last year."

Charles sighed heavily.

"He's also checking out commercial real estate." I looked down at my watch. I needed to change for the afternoon, thinking about my coffee date with Michel. "Charles I should get ready for class. Please look into what you can do."

When I hung up, I realized I would also need to figure out what I could do.

* * * *

"Now that we are all warmed up, we'll listen to Mr. Jerome play "Valse Lente" and then the second time, I will dance to it."

It was back to business after the ordeal early this morning. I nodded to Jerome to begin. I watched as the children's eyes lit up to the music. Then I danced, my leg just the slightest bit sore, taking steps that they would learn in the following weeks. After I finished, all of the children clapped.

"Okay, everyone, starting with your feet in first position and holding your arms in front as in an oval, move your arms smoothly into second position. Plié. Wonderful! Stretch your right leg forward with a gliding feeling. Remember your basic positions should be performed precisely with feeling and expression. Right arm up, lift your eyes and follow your hand. Beautiful. Now let's take tiny steps to the right, skimming across the room..."

As the children followed the routine, I glanced out the window and saw Michel watching the class, snowflakes falling on his head and shoulders. I had almost cancelled with him. I needed to know more about the cause of Stephen's death, but I didn't think I should cancel our date. Coffee wouldn't take long. Of course then there was dinner with Todd and Monica.

"... floating. You should look like you're floating. Beautiful!"

After class was over and all the children had performed their reverence, they started to disperse. Michel entered the studio, stamping his feet on the rug by the door.

Jerome had a surprised look on his face when I introduced Michel to him. I had forgotten to tell Jerome that I was meeting with Michel after class. I was sure I would be hearing from him soon, as to why the shocked look. Jerome was a dear friend who always told me what he thought. I treasured having a friend like him, especially one from way back.

Michel and I conversed amicably as we walked to Back to Eden Bakery and ordered coffee at the counter when we arrived. I declined a dessert wanting to save my appetite for dinner this evening.

We sat by the window. "Well, here's one infamous window that I saw you through. Funny how I have seen you so often."

He laughed. My mind started thinking of the many times I had. It was uncanny.

He stirred sugar into his coffee and then took a bite of his carrot cake. "So Irina, tell me about yourself. Do you have any children?"

I put my coffee down and hesitated a moment. Rather odd to ask about children as a first question. "No...I haven't."

He looked down and fiddled with his fork.

I returned the question. "Do you have any children? Are you married?"

"No. Never had the time to settle down. I've moved a lot with my career, first with schooling and then work. I've lived in several cities in Europe. This is my first time in the United States."

"Where have you all lived? Tell me about yourself."

As I listened to Michel, early on I discovered we connected easily and related well to each other. We were more alike than different. We had much in common, art, music, and surprisingly ballet, no lack of things to talk about. I knew I was going to like him.

"I was adopted and my adopted parents are both gone now, my mother died last year."

"I'm sorry. I know how hard losing a parent can be. My parents are gone also. I think about them often."

"So you must have travelled in Europe with your company and have exciting stories about all the people you met."

Thinking about the time and that I wanted to look up information regarding Stephen, I responded, "I've met lots of interesting people. I suppose the highlight was dancing in Lithuania, where my parents were born."

"Interesting." We chatted a bit about Lithuania, my performances there.

"Did you meet anyone special?"

Anyone special? This again was an unusual question. "I made many special friends overseas, some I still keep in touch with."

"I mean in Lithuania, your nationality."

I knew I was being ambiguous. Why did he even want to know any of this? I suppose to make conversation. Sometimes people were uncomfortable with lulls.

I finished my coffee. "I hate to be rude but I'm afraid I'm going to have to cut our visit short. Something unexpected came up. I almost had to cancel coffee."

"May I call on you again?"

"I'd like that very much. Thank you for the coffee and being so understanding. I had a wonderful time visiting with you."

* * * *

When I arrived home, a message from Charles was on voice-mail. I called him back.

"They still haven't done an autopsy? Time's running short. This morning I read online about specific tests on hair that can be run to detect high levels of metals that would indicate a person having been poisoned."

"So you think, Stephen was poisoned. Do you have proof?" Charles asked.

"Of course I don't. I suspect it. It would explain everything. That's why an autopsy needs to be done."

"Irina, for now let the police handle this. If the coroner doesn't think there is justification for an autopsy and you feel strongly about this, you could get an approval from the D.A. who then would need the approval of a judge."

"Sounds like a long process. Time we don't have. Why aren't the police investigating? A young man dies suddenly. That should be enough suspicion."

"His wife said he had been sickly."

I sighed. "She could be the murderer. Her and her dark sister."

"Be careful making any accusations. Are you willing to start a lawsuit to do this? Just saying. There isn't any evidence to back up what you suspect."

"That's why we need an autopsy. Please see if there is anything you can do about this. Convince them about the autopsy."

"Irina, you know I'd do anything for you. Trying and succeeding are very different. You may have to contact a lawyer to guide you through this."

"I have you to guide me."

Charles didn't respond.

"I'll try and come up with some evidence, I said."

He then let out a sigh. "Be careful. If what you think is true, prying could be dangerous."

* * * *

On our way to meet up with Monica and Todd in the Village, Robert and I talked about Stephen and then about my coffee date with Michel.

"If there is in fact a murderer," Robert said, "the police will eventually find him. Do you suspect anyone?"

"No." I hesitated. "Not really. I'm hoping they'll do an autopsy soon to determine the cause of death."

The taxi driver adjusted his rear view mirror, his eyes meeting mine after I said that.

"And this young man you met up with today, I don't think you should encourage him. You don't know if he has good intentions."

Intentions? "I've always been a good judge of character."

"What did you talk to a perfect stranger about?"

What a strange question and attitude Robert had. The taxi driver looked at me again in the mirror with a half-smirk on his face. It seemed as if he was waiting for an answer also as he pulled in front of the restaurant. "Books we've read, art, music. We had a lot in common. He loves ballet."

Robert paid the driver then said, "Sounds like he's quite interested in you. I still think you shouldn't encourage him."

I shook my head as we walked into my favorite Thai Asian Fusion restaurant.

We greeted Monica and Todd by way of hugs and double-cheeked air kisses. At least I did. Monica more or less pressed her body up against Robert's while Todd and I exchanged pleasantries. *But then she had always been more Robert's friend in college than mine.* I felt like I was watching some grand seduction. What did Todd think? Better yet, what was Robert thinking?

Monica had held up well for her age. I squinted, trying to decide whether she had had a facelift or not and stopped when I realized what I was doing. Perhaps the overpowering perfume she bathed herself in acted as a preservative. Her hair was in a short bob with blunt bangs. Décolletage burst out of her plunging lacy vanilla dress which contrasted my basic black dress with clean lines. I had added a scarf for a touch of color. Todd had a warm smile that continued up to his eyes.

We waited for several minutes before being shown to our table next to a window. After looking over the menu, we ordered a few appetizers.

"Irina, what have you been up to?" Monica asked. "I haven't seen you in ages. I hear you've settled for teaching young children ballet. Do you expect them to become ballerinas under your tutelage?"

"Oh...children have their dreams. I am guiding them to become the better of whoever they turn out to be. They'll have poise and grace and will grow in confidence and esteem."

Monica arched a well-groomed eyebrow and looked over at Robert.

Robert mentioned we had just been at the Impressionist Exhibition.

"You always were into art," Monica said. "Wasn't that your major before you quit university?"

I was about to respond when Monica blurted out, "Did you ever manage to get a degree? Dancers are not known for...well you know...how can they study with all that dancing?"

Monica was indeed an unlikable woman.

"Somewhat true. Irina couldn't handle both her studies and her ballet. She had to make a choice," Robert said.

I couldn't believe this conversation. I had received a full scholarship to NYU having done well academically in high school even with my grueling ballet training.

Robert seeing my reaction added, "She chose wisely."

"Irina, what a wonderful career you've had." Todd saved the awkward situation. He brushed his hair back with his hand. He must have noticed the edge Monica projected in her remarks. "I've followed you over the years, your ballet company."

I smiled. I liked Todd. Again, before I had a chance to respond, Monica blurted out, "So Robert, when is your son coming to New York?"

I turned to Robert. "You didn't tell me your son was visiting?"

Robert looked up towards the ceiling. "It must have escaped my mind. It's just for a couple of days."

"I'd love to meet him. Which son is it?"

A glint of sweat appeared on Robert's forehead.

"Theo. He's a civil engineer," Monica responded with a grin that I wanted to wipe off her face. "He looks so much like Samantha. But he has your sense of humor and intellect." Monica glanced at me with her fake smile.

Todd looked at Monica and cleared his throat. "I'd be interested in seeing the Impressionist exhibition. I haven't been to The Met in a while."

"A bit stuffy, but you *might* enjoy it," Robert said to Todd unbuttoning the top button of his shirt and loosening his tie.

Stuffy? That threw me for a loop. I thought *he had* enjoyed the exhibition which was *truly incredible*. We had such a great time together there. How little did I really know of Robert? I was happy when our appetizers arrived.

Monica took a bite of the Thai shrimp. "I haven't been here in ages," Monica said before swallowing her food. Her eyes went wide. She then drank a half glass of water. It must have been too spicy.

"Spicy?" Robert asked.

"I'm fine." She took another drink. "We've quite outgrown always going to Thai restaurants a few years out of college."

I looked over at Robert. I felt like standing up and leaving right then and there. I caught myself before I replied and said something ugly.

Robert wiped his mouth in his cloth napkin. "I've been meaning to take Irina to Le Chateau."

"Le Chateau is a favorite restaurant of ours," Monica said looking starry-eyed. "Elegant dining, pairing wines from France." Her voice went up a half-octave.

I smiled trying to make the most of it. "Sounds lovely."

"You'd love it, Irina. The tables are next to paintings by the masters, Picasso, Dali, and others," Todd said.

"And their Ile Flottante is to die for," Monica said.

Monica smiled, looking between Robert and me. "Irina, a floating island," she added.

"I know what Ile Fottante is."

Todd put his fork down on his plate. "This chicken satay is to die for."

"I agree," turning my attention to Todd. "This is my favorite restaurant in the Village." I hesitated, "In all of Manhattan, in fact." I enjoyed French food also. What was with Robert's demeaning attitude? And Monica...so boorish. Why did I let this woman get to me? Was it because she knew Robert's son was visiting and I didn't? I expected more from Robert.

Monica looked up at Robert and smiled, then she took a sly glance at her reflection in the window, for the second time I noted, primping her hair.

Cutting into a piece of fried eggplant, I decided my conversation with Monica was over.

Robert might have finally sensed my appalling disgust and decided to initiate further conversation. "Monica, tell Irina about the Sway Arts Initiative."

Monica moved her food around with her pinkie raised effortlessly skyward. "I'm a principal fundraiser for the Sway Arts Initiative. Perhaps you've seen my photo in the New York Observer at the American Ballet Theater's 75th Anniversary."

"I rarely read the Observer." I was a subscriber.

Monica winced.

Our entrées arrived. I took a bite of my roasted duck in Kaneng Kua curry sauce and closed my eyes to savor the taste, the texture. Perhaps mindfulness would get me through this horrible evening, giving my attention fully to my food. I opened my eyes.

Robert had ordered the red curry and drank water between each bite. Todd seemed to be enjoying his marinated pork chop, while Monica moved her crab fried rice around the plate. Clearly this wasn't the restaurant Robert should have chosen.

After a dessert of fried banana with ice cream, of course ice cream was too plebeian for Monica, Robert paid the bill. When Robert said we should do this again, before parting ways, I couldn't help myself and turned away rolling my eyes. A waiter caught me doing it and smiled. Monica suggested "a better restaurant."

Hailing a taxi, Robert said, "Wasn't that pleasant? Monica and Todd are delightful, aren't they? You seemed to get along well with them."

At first I thought it best not to respond. I'd never have a repeat performance, although Todd was amazing, amazing that he was with Monica. But then I said, "Yes, I've always found *learning* pleasant and I did learn a lot tonight."

While travelling home, I thought about Robert not telling me about his son visiting. Why hadn't he? Had he simply forgot? And Monica. I could see she had some kind of a history with Robert, other than being friends in college. At this point, I wasn't sure I even cared.

By the time we arrived back at my brownstone, my thoughts had gone back to Stephen. What if an autopsy wasn't ordered by the medical examiner? Was I, and perhaps Margarite, the only persons who thought something wasn't quite right with his death? One day had already passed. What if Tricia had Stephen cremated?

Chapter Ten

While sitting in the kitchen drinking coffee, looking at a trailing English ivy on my counter, I suddenly remembered...the plants! There had been six herbal plants on Alice's windowsill and I only saw four yesterday morning. What happened to the other two plants? Stephen had mentioned that Tricia always provided him with herbal supplements. I had even helped Stephen stuff the brown paper bag, that held an herbal drink Tricia had given him, into his overnight case. I bet he threw the health shake away knowing he wouldn't get it through the airline security.

Was this why Stephen was looking so poorly these past few weeks and he looked better when he came back from his trip? Could his food have been tainted even poisoned by those plants? Had Alice and Tricia simply gotten rid of the evidence? The plants? The poison? And this was why they were so set against an autopsy? If my loved one had died, I would definitely want to know the exact cause. Oh, my, God. What did the plants look like again? Could I even remember if I saw a photo of them?

Thank goodness, Robert hadn't stayed over. He had suggested it, but I feigned a headache, feeling I needed to reevaluate our relationship after yesterday evening's fiasco. But that would have to wait. I sat at the edge of my bed, closed my eyes, smiled, and took a deep breath through my nose and exhaled through my mouth. Then repeated it, bringing my focus to the present moment as I had learned studying mindfulness. I tried clearing away all thoughts of Robert. I jumped out of bed. I needed to act fast and find out where those plants disappeared to. Time was ticking away.

I knocked on Tricia's door. As I stood waiting, I could faintly smell Monica's perfume on me. There's nothing worse, than hugging someone who "bathes" in scent and then smelling like they do afterwards. It must be in my hair. I'd need to take a shower.

Alice answered. She shook her head and walked away, back into their apartment, leaving the door ajar.

I couldn't believe how rude Alice was. Well, actually I could.

Tricia came to the door and smiled. "Hello, Irina. You'll have to excuse Alice first thing in the morning. She's not a morning person."

I'll say she's not and she's not an afternoon or evening person either. "Good morning, Tricia. I wanted to find out how you are doing?" Tricia looked chipper enough.

Her eyes moistened. Then she looked down. "I'm hanging in there. It's still difficult to believe Stephen's gone."

Almost as a reflex, I reached out and took her hand in mine. "Is there something I can help you with?"

With a grave expression she said, "Not really. We bagged all of Stephen's things and plan to donate them to the Salvation Army next week."

That was quick. I looked past Tricia around the room.

"They're in my bedroom. Would you like to come in?"

"Sure, for a few minutes."

Entering their dimmed living room, I glanced at the plants on the windowsill. Tricia followed my eyes and walked over to the windows and lifted the cellular shades by the plants. "We slept in. I haven't had time to open the shades yet." She then opened the second shade.

"Your plants, they look so healthy. Didn't you have more herbal plants here the other day? I notice some are missing."

Alice walked into the room carrying a coffee mug. "My aren't you observant. Two had spider mites. We had to get rid of them."

So Alice had been listening to our conversation. "What herbs were they?"

Tricia interrupted. "Where are my manners? Irina would you like a cup of coffee? I just made a pot."

The way Alice looked at Tricia, squinting, seemed to me like some kind of message. Perhaps she was trying to say to Tricia, why prolong my visit?

I pursed my lips. "Sure, that would be great." I wanted to follow Tricia into the kitchen when Alice spoke.

"Rau Răm."

"Pardon."

Alice sighed heavily with a pinched expression. "Rau Răm. Vietnamese coriander. Haven't you ever used it?"

"I've used coriander many times, but I've never seen the plant."

Alice's eyes widened. "Why all this interest in our herbs?"

"I might try and grow some. I have a great window for them as well."

Tricia came back from the kitchen and handed me the coffee. "I wouldn't bother with the coriander. Easier to buy that herb at the grocery store."

I put the cup down on the coffee table. "Stephen had been ill for a while. I noticed after he was gone to the conference and returned he looked much better."

"You talked to him?" Tricia asked.

"Yes. He seemed almost back to his healthy self."

Alice cocked her head to one side and said with a sneer, "What are you getting at?"

I picked up the cup of steaming coffee and looked at it. "Nothing. Just an observation. Would you mind if I added a little milk to the coffee?"

"I'll take your cup," Tricia said.

"I'll come with you,"I said quickly before Alice said anything else.

I followed Tricia into the kitchen. While she went to the refrigerator to get the milk, I noticed a pile of mail, magazines, and other miscellaneous items spread out on their counter that hadn't been there Thursday evening when their kitchen was spotless.

Tricia took a quart of milk out of their refrigerator. I needed some excuse to look around.

"Tricia would you mind if I used your bathroom, otherwise I could go back to my apartment?"

"Don't be silly. Of course you can use the bathroom. I'll add some milk and take your coffee into the living room."

"I'll just be a few minutes."

I walked down the hallway. Turning around I saw Tricia go back into the living room carrying the coffee. I glanced into Tricia's bedroom. Sure enough, several large black garbage bags were leaning against the wall. Passing Stephen's office, I saw a number of papers scattered on his desk. I went into the bathroom, closed the door, and quietly opened the medicine chest looking for Stephen's comb or hairbrush. I wanted to get a sample of his hair for drug testing. Nothing. I flushed the toilet and turned on the faucets.

Closing the door to the bathroom, I went across the hall to the office. I glanced at the papers, then quietly started opening drawers. In the bottom drawer were divorce papers. Oh my God! Stephen's signature was on them. Tricia's wasn't. I thought he was just talking to a lawyer. Had Tricia known about these papers? Was I now staring at some kind of a motive for murder? Did Tricia kill Stephen because of the divorce papers? Or her crazy sister or both? Did Alice talk Tricia into poisoning Stephen? Was I jumping to conclusions? Was that why he was looking so poorly? My mind was racing. Tricia would lose much with a divorce.

I started looking for a life insurance policy on Stephen until I heard footsteps coming down the hall. I quickly closed the drawer and crouched down behind the desk. When the steps retreated back into the living room, I rushed into the bathroom and turned off the faucets.

"Sorry about that," I said coming back into the living room. I went out last night and have a bit of an upset stomach."

"Irina, Stephen's funeral is next Friday. We hate to wait that long, but Stephen's sister can't arrive until Thursday. She lives in Australia."

Six days should give me some time to find a reason for an autopsy to be done.

"A while back Stephen and I talked about if anything ever happened to us. Stephen's wish was to be cremated."

Maybe not six days. Young, healthy people talking about death and cremation? It didn't seem likely to me. I looked down at my coffee, thinking of the herbal plants, I didn't feel safe drinking it. Especially thinking Stephen might have been poisoned or at least given something that made him sick. I faked taking a sip.

Was it my imagination or were both Tricia and Alice watching me take that sip?

"I hope you'll be able to make it," Tricia hesitated, "to the funeral that is."

Strange. Of course I would come. Stephen was my friend. I looked over at Alice. She sat with her legs crossed smiling one of her rare smiles. I was getting even more paranoid now with Alice smiling at me.

Tricia added, "Odd that our friend Alex Rankin asked if we could hold it sooner. "

Our friend. I thought he was Stephen's business associate. I didn't know he was Tricia's friend as well.

"Alex has to leave on a business trip Thursday evening for several days, but it just isn't possible."

Putting the cup down on the coffee table, I stood up. Their eyes seemed to follow the cup. "If there's anything I can do for you, Tricia, please let me know."

"Thank you, that's very kind, but I'm in good hands with Alice here.

I looked over at Alice. She now had a perfunctory smile on her face.

"Glad to hear it."

Alice stood up. "It's a shame you didn't get to finish your coffee?"

Did Alice know what I was thinking and was she just trying to freak me out? "I have a date with Margarite and need to get ready."

* * * *

Margarite and I exited the taxi and started walking the half block down 5th Avenue for our appointment with a professional fundraiser regarding the proceeds.

"There were divorce papers in his bottom desk drawer. That could be a motive for murder."

"Irina, come on. I was served with divorce papers, Margarite said. "My ex-husband's still alive." She smiled then chuckled opening her mouth to add something then closed it. I bet it was the word "unfortunately." There was no love lost between her and her ex-husband since he had left her for his young "bimbo", as Margarite so often put it.

"Perhaps Stephen told Tricia, rather he insisted, that Alice leave or the alternative was divorce. Having the papers showed he meant business. Tricia in turn might have told Alice and murder was Alice's revenge."

We stopped to view the exquisite window display at Tiffany & Co. "Would you like to go in?"

Margarite looked at her watch. "Better not. Perhaps after the meeting."

We lingered a couple of minutes longer gazing at the jewelry. A sterling silver, double cuff bracelet caught my eye.

"Tricia mentioned yesterday they were going to cremate Stephen. You have people cremated if you don't want an autopsy done. This makes everything more urgent. I wonder how well insured Stephen was. I wish I had found a policy."

"I imagine even through his work Stephen was well insured," Margarite said, "and you were taking a big chance looking around."

"I'm sure you're right about the policy." And the chance. "Stephen would have known that if anything happened to him, Trisha wouldn't make it in New York City with her job. If Stephen had gotten a divorce, he probably would have changed the beneficiary on his life insurance at work or any other policies he may have had, to someone else. Financially, it would be better for Tricia to end their marriage with death rather than a divorce." A shiver ran down my spine after I said this.

Margarite shook her head. "Such horrid thoughts."

We continued walking and entered the tower building next door.

* * * *

"I can't believe it, nearly $25,000 raised when all is said and done," Margarite said smiling large, her eyes sparkling.

"This is going to mean so much for our programs."

Before we left for home, we decided to celebrate and have coffee and pastries on the second level of the tower. I told Margarite about my thoughts of Tricia and Alice poisoning Stephen with the plants. "How would I know if those were really herbal plants? I plan to check the garbage to see if I can find them."

111

"So you've decided then that Tricia and Alice definitely poisoned Stephen?" Margarite asked, taking a bite of her glazed apricot tart.

"I don't know. I haven't decided on anything. Right now that's all I've got."

"Do you ever think that it is a bit of a coincidence that both Robert and Michel show up around the same time that Stephen died?"

I put down my fork. The cranberry streusel was to die for. "No. That never crossed my mind. What are you getting at?"

Margarite shrugged. "Nothing, really. Back to Tricia and Alice, If you thought they poisoned Stephen with the missing herbs, you should have gone through their garbage as soon as you left their apartment." Margarite started laughing. "Although I can't visualize you searching through garbage cans, a former soloist in the New York Ballet."

I took a sip of my coffee. "Funny, Margarite!"

"Sorry! And with all of your mention of plants, if they were indeed poisonous, Tricia and Alice would have gotten rid of them as soon as you left."

"I'm definitely not looking forward to the adventure, but that's exactly what I plan to do."

Margarite laughed again. "I hope your students' mothers don't see you or worse yet, someone sees you, snaps a photo of you picking through the garbage, and you're in a scandalous article in the New York Post."

I shook my head. "I still have the keys to their apartment that I used when they were away on vacation. This was before Alice showed up on the scene. Tricia told me to keep the keys in case of an emergency."

Margarite's voice became more serious. "What are you suggesting?"

"That Stephen's death is an emergency."

"Irina..."

I finished my coffee and looked straight ahead. "I may have to."

* * * *

I came up with the excuse that I might have accidentally thrown away a drug prescription, should anyone see me digging through the garbage cans kept outside of the basement apartment. While searching, I found nothing other than an expensive, unusual looking water bottle and a distinctive blue checked shirt of Stephen's that I hoped I could find a hair sample from. Putting both into a paper bag I had placed near the garbage cans, I came up the small stairway and took a chance and looked through the garbage cans at the brownstone next door.

In the first can, halfway down, I found a small paper bag that contained pieces of a unique emerald green Murano glass vase. It had tiny white flowers painted on gold filigree. It was Margarite's. She had bought the vase on a trip to Italy. I had just admired the piece a couple of weeks ago. Perhaps she had broken the vase, but because of the home burglaries occurring in the area, I kept it out. I'd ask Margarite about it later. And if she did throw it away, why would she have thrown it in the neighbor's garbage?

I heard a door close. Our neighbor, Celeste from upstairs came out of the brownstone next door, carrying a large canvas bag. I huddled down behind the garbage cans not wanting her to see me. I would have been so embarrassed and now having a large bag of garbage collected, it would have been hard to say I was looking for a piece of paper. After she passed and hustled up the stairs into our building, I came out of hiding and continued my search.

Deep in the bottom of the second garbage can I found both plants. I remembered what the pots looked like. The plants looked half dead. Why would Alice have thrown the plants into the neighbor's garbage cans? I tore the plants out of the dirt and put them in a second paper bag I had brought

113

along and hurried up the stairs of my brownstone with the two bags. When I glanced at Tricia's window, I saw a shadow move.

Back in my apartment after thoroughly washing my hands, even though I had donned kitchen gloves, I called Jerome at home and told him the situation. Besides volunteering as a pianist for my ballet studio, Jerome was a semi-retired, research investigator at NYU in the biochemistry department. He gave me a friend's name that worked at NYU in the Plant Biology Department and said he'd go over with me later to deliver the plants.

"It's quite suspicious that they would have been in the garbage cans at the brownstone next door and not in our own."

"Odd, but then you said the mystery writer is odd. Irina, by the way, I've been wondering who this Michel is?"

I sat down on the sofa. "Someone I recently met." I laughed. "I literally fell for him." I told Jerome about slipping down my front steps.

"Don't you notice anything about the way he looks?"

"You mean that he's incredibly handsome?" I laughed again. "You're taken."

He laughed. "You haven't noticed the resemblance?"

My brows pulled in. "Resemblance?" I thought for a few moments not saying anything. "He looks familiar to me, but then I've seen him so many times around the neighborhood, that could be why."

Jerome sounded surprised. "Irina, he looks like he could be your younger brother. You have so many of the same features. Are you sure your parents didn't have a second child?"

I shook my head. Jerome was always fabricating things. "Seriously, next time you see him, take a good look."

I could visualize Michel right now. Changing the subject, I told Jerome about Robert and our dinner out with Monica and Todd.

"She's a real bitch, isn't she?" Jerome said.

"I'm in total agreement. She *is*."

Jerome laughed again. "I never did see what Robert saw in her. But don't worry, she and Robert are definitely in the past."

Frowning I said, "I thought Robert's wife just died?"

"Irina, your imagination is running wild seeing them as an item."

I never said I saw them as an item. However, Monica was all over Robert in front of Todd.

"I wouldn't have gotten the two of you together had Monica been in the picture."

"I'm beginning to think it was a mistake, Robert and me."

"Don't say that. Monica means nothing to him. All he talks about is you."

I sighed. "It's not only Monica. I didn't like the direction of the conversation yesterday evening."

Did Jerome even see Robert or talk to him all that much? Robert never once mentioned Jerome or talked about wanting to get together with him. How close were they, really?

"Irina, I wouldn't say this if I didn't think it could happen again for you and Robert. Give him a chance. Give yourself a chance, to be happy."

"I am happy! I have been happy!"

Chapter Eleven

Sunday, February 22

That afternoon Alice had an author event at the Corner Bookstore on Madison Avenue, which put Tricia and Alice out of their apartment for a few hours. Margarite and I had been invited to her book reading. Perhaps she didn't have many friends to invite. We both came up with excuses.

"I can't believe you talked me into this," Margarite said. "If anyone gets wind of us..." Margarite hesitated. "Well, I suppose if Tricia and Alice possibly poisoned Stephen, this is a necessary evil."

I took Tricia's keys out of a covered wicker basket I kept on a shelf in the kitchen. "This might be our only chance. We need to take advantage of their being gone."

"Oh, my gosh, I'm glad I'm not at the bookstore. Serial killers, gore, and creepiness is definitely her forte."

I shook my head. "Sometimes I wonder about authors who are even able to write content like that. Are their minds dark and twisted like their stories?"

Margarite flinched. "Alice is definitely a peculiar person."

"Stephen might be alive had she not moved in with Tricia and him." After I said that I had a hollow feeling in the pit of my stomach.

Before we left my apartment I opened the bag holding Margarite's Venetian vase. "I found this in our neighbor's garbage can."

Margarite's eyes opened wide. "That's my vase! It's broken! How did it get there?"

"So you didn't throw it away?"

"No. I didn't even know it was missing." Her face reddened. "Someone took it from my apartment. I wonder what else is missing? I'm calling the police. I've been burgled!"

"Can't you wait until we finish breaking into—"

She crossed her arms. "You mean going into..."

"Right. Of course. That's what I meant. Can't you wait until we *go* into Tricia's apartment? Remember this is an emergency. We're justified in searching their apartment. Think of Stephen. He deserves the truth. He deserves closure."

She tilted her head. "Then, why don't I have a good feeling about this?"

I shrugged. Morally I felt fine with entering their apartment. My crusading spirit for justice was high.

We went out in the hall just as our neighbor, Celeste from upstairs, was coming in the front door carrying a couple of paper grocery bags.

"Hello there. I thought you two might be at Alice's book signing," she said.

"Didn't think we could make it," I responded. "There's lots going on this afternoon."

She laughed and started going up the stairs. "You, also. That was my excuse."

We returned to my apartment until we heard her door close.

Margarite peeked out into the hall and said quickly, "All is clear. Let's keep your apartment unlocked in case we need a quick escape."

I hesitated a bit not really wanting to keep my door unlocked thinking about Margarite's theft. "I don't know. I'm not comfortable leaving it open." I hesitated several moments. "Well, all right. We won't be gone long."

We entered Tricia's apartment and locked the door from the inside. I showed Margarite the windowsill with the plants. "You can still see the water marks."

"Irina, I don't want to be here any longer than necessary talking about rings on the woodwork."

"Okay. Let's start in the office where I found the divorce papers."

We entered the office. Papers were laying across the top of the desk. I looked through them thoroughly and then went to the bottom drawer. "The divorce papers were in this drawer. They aren't here any longer. Tricia or Alice must have taken them."

"And possibly destroyed them."

Looking through each drawer carefully, I didn't find the divorce papers or anything out of the ordinary. Just the usual bills, receipts, restaurant menus, greeting cards. No life insurance policy. "This is really disappointing."

Margarite looked at her watch. "I should have my head examined for being here." She bit at her lip. "We must be nuts. *I* must be nuts."

"Let's see if we can find something in the kitchen."

She smirked. "Like a bottle with a skull and cross bones on it?"

"Exactly." I turned and started walking towards the kitchen.

Margarite followed. "I thought you said Stephen was poisoned with the herbal plants."

"That isn't definite until the report comes back."

"What report? You mean the autopsy that hasn't been ordered?"

I didn't respond. In a lower kitchen cabinet next to a partially used case of energy drinks, we found large bottles of organic protein plant-based powder, sport performance protein, and 100% whey protein.

One bottle read "to fuel lean muscle tissue."

"Stephen was definitely into body building," Margarite noted.

Along side these was a plastic box filled with at least a dozen bottles containing pills. Margarite and I looked through them.

"These are nootropics. Some of these my ex-husband used. Brain-boosting drugs. Never did much for him."

I smiled, wondering if perhaps Margarite should go to counseling to alleviate some of her hostility towards her Ex. "There are so many bottles with just a few capsules left. This one reads for Memory, Focus, and Energy." I put it back in the box. "I read an article about young executives, the white-collar elite, using chemical assistance for focus and to enhance creativity."

"They are starting to be as acceptable as coffee," Margarite said.

I took in a deep breath. "Had Stephen been over-medicating with cognitive-enhancing drugs? Do you suppose he might have in fact caused his own death with these brain-boosters?"

"That never dawned on me, but it's a good theory," Margarite said with a pensive expression. "Even some high school students have been found to use them at my school. We call them 'smart drugs.'"

"Stephen was juggling a lot. Work, competition for a promotion, home, Tricia, Alice, social networking. He must have thought he needed the exact boost," I said.

"Maybe he overdosed."

I took the pen and paper next to the phone and wrote down the names of the supplements. "Have I been wrong about Tricia and Alice all along? I'm surprised Tricia didn't throw these out when she packed up Stephen's clothes. She must have known about them."

Margarite shrugged. "She might use them also. Or Alice with her writing."

"I wonder if there are others in their master bathroom. The main bathroom didn't have any when I looked in the medicine cabinet."

While in the kitchen, we heard a quiet knock on the apartment door. As we tiptoed to the door, there was a second soft knocking. I peeked just for a second into the peephole and saw Celeste looking in the direction of the front door. What was she doing here? She knew Tricia and Alice were gone. She turned the handle to the door jiggling it and I heard scratching noises. My heart started racing.

I looked over at Margarite who mouthed "Now what?" Next the outside front door of the brownstone opened and I heard people talking. I hoped it wasn't Tricia and Alice. My heart now raced in double time.

"What's going on?" Margarite whispered with a pained look.

I looked through the peephole again when I heard retreating footsteps in the hallway. "Celeste is leaving, walking towards the front door," I whispered back. "What was that about? Celeste checking the door to see if it was locked?"

"I don't know. Perhaps Celeste thought Tricia and Alice were back already." She ran a jerky hand through her hair. "Let's get out of here."

"We are almost done. I need to check the master bathroom to see if we can find Stephen's hairbrush for a hair sample so it can be tested for poison. There wasn't one in the main bathroom cabinet the other day."

"Well, let's hurry up," she said, clasping her hands together.

We searched both bathrooms and Tricia and Stephen's bedroom. We didn't find a hairbrush, only a few more bottles of the nootropics under a stack of hand towels. "His clothes," I said.

The bags of clothing were still against the wall in the bedroom. His hair brush was either thrown away or in those bags. I felt around the bags for something hard, then carefully untwisted the ties to the first bag and looked through it the best I could without removing everything. I found a couple of sweaters and on one, short blonde hairs. It was definitely not Tricia's or Alice's hair. "Margarite, could you please get a baggie out of the kitchen. I saw a box in the drawer next to the stove."

When she came back, I put the hair into the bag using a tissue. I didn't want to contaminate it with my DNA. I didn't even know if that was possible or not, but I didn't want to take a chance. "Okay, let's leave now."

"Aren't you curious about Alice's bedroom?" Margarite asked with raised eyebrows. "What evil lurks in it?"

My eyebrows drew together. "I thought you were in a big hurry to leave."

"Just one peek as long as we're here. It will only take a second. We'll never get the opportunity again."

Margarite walked down the hall and opened the door. "Oh, my, God."

"What? What is it?"

"I can't believe it."

I looked into the room, then laughed. "It's modern, neutral, all clean lines like the rest of Tricia's apartment. Oh, you mean the poster." A life-size poster of Tom Jones hung on the wall.

"Her taste."

I laughed again. "Scary. Let's leave."

As we left, I patted the baggie I had placed in my pants pocket.

After we exited the apartment, Margarite went directly to her apartment to start dinner. That evening she was having a teacher friend over who was going through chemotherapy.

I made a cup of tea to calm my nerves and then called Charles at work. "I have a sample of Stephen's hair."

"How did you get it? No. No, Irina on second thought don't tell me."

"I can come down to the station in a little while."

I heard a quiet sigh. "Bring it first thing in the morning?"

"I know this is a big favor. Will you be able to send it to the lab right away?"

"I'll see you tomorrow, Irina."

After hanging up with Charles, I thought about Robert and decided to take Jerome's advice and give Robert another chance. I hadn't heard from him since Friday evening when I didn't talk much on the way back from dinner. I thought it over and perhaps I was too hard on him for not telling me about his son visiting. I'd surprise him.

I went to Zabar's and picked up a few things: different cheeses, fruit, a small container of olives, a baguette, and a bottle of wine. It would be interesting to see his new apartment, his decorating style. I could suggest helping him with the furnishings. That would be fun.

It took about twenty minutes to walk to Robert's apartment. He lived close to Riverside Boulevard. All the way there I thought about what I would say when he answered the door. Something clever? Something sweet? As I arrived at Robert's high-rise condominium, I noticed there was a group of people gathered at the entrance. They were waiting for a doorman who was holding open the door for an elderly lady taking her Westie out for a walk. "I'm sorry madam, but I don't have time to walk your dog," he said to her.

I entered the posh lobby with several children holding brightly wrapped gifts, their mothers beside them. Another group of children were already in the lobby. I walked past them and rode the elevator up with some of the excited children to the 10th floor. When I got off, I smiled and said, "Have a fun day, children!"

They responded in unison, "We will," and giggled.

I found Robert's door, knocked, and gathered my thoughts. When Robert opened the door, I could hear voices coming from inside. "Irina, what a surprise. What are you doing here?"

I handed him the bag. "I thought I'd surprise you with an early supper. But if you're busy..."

He took the bag. "How nice," Robert said smiling, but his eyes didn't connect with that smile.

I peered past Robert. "Sounds like you have company."

A flush crept along his cheeks. "I do. Well, come in."

"I can come back at another time."

"Of course not." He looked down at the bag. "Not after you've gone to all of this trouble."

I followed Robert through the narrow entryway into a spacious kitchen where he put the food. Entering the living room, I found Monica chatting away amicably with a man sitting on the sofa. I should have realized she was in the apartment by her overused scent.

"Hello Irina," Monica said. "Nice to see you again." Monica didn't look like she was at all happy to see me. "I didn't know Robert invited you to *our* little party."

Robert took my coat and scarf in his arms and mumbled, "Irina, it's not really a party." He then introduced me to the person sitting next to Monica. "Irina, this is my son Theo. Theo, this is Irina, the ballet teacher I told you about. We were friends in college."

"Oh, you must have known Dad when he was a hippie."

Ballet teacher? Friends in college? I smiled. "Nice to meet you, Theo. I heard you were coming to visit. I didn't realize it was so soon."

"I've had my ticket for months now since Dad moved to Manhattan. Nice to meet you. Was it, Irine?"

Theo had no idea who I was. And Robert had been here for months. I looked over at Robert. His face was even more red now. He put my scarf on top of my coat and walked down a hallway with them. Monica's imminent smirk arrived. "Her name is Irina."

Robert always seemed to be holding something back. I wanted to leave.

"Irina, please have a seat," Theo said.

I sat down in an Eames lounge chair across from Monica. As I noted the ease of the chair, trying to find comfort in anything, I glanced out Robert's wall of window which afforded a gorgeous view of the Hudson River.

I looked back at Theo, and smiled when he said, "So you know Monica, another friend of Dad's. She's been like an aunt to me and my brother."

Robert came back into the room and pulled out a chair that was in the corner. "Irina, Theo's flight came in this morning."

I continued smiling. "Monica and I are acquaintances."

"Theo's thinking of possibly moving here," Monica said. "Wouldn't that be fabulous." She turned to Theo and patted his leg. "Then I wouldn't have to wait for several months between visits."

So Theo, and I'm sure Robert, had been to New York City many times previously.

Theo looked at me. "My son goes to Cornell."

Taken back that he would already have a son in college, I raised my eyebrows and said, "You look so young to have a son in college."

Monica looked at me and smiled. "Theo's forty. You'd never guess it. Such young looking skin, just like his father's."

"My son is a freshman," Theo said.

My mouth was getting tired from nonstop smiling. I glanced over at Robert. He looked uncomfortable tugging at his shirt sleeves.

He glanced at me, then quickly changed the subject. "Irina, I thought perhaps you and I could take Theo to a play this week. 'Disaster' is playing at the Nederlander Theatre. The reviews say it's quite hilarious."

Being here was a disaster. My thoughts were as busy as Grand Central Station at rush hour. Forty. Then it hit me. Theo would have been born the year Robert graduated from college and left for San Francisco. We lived together until he left in June. The bright light of his modern apartment suddenly dimmed.

"Irina, you've gone pale," Monica said.

"I'm sorry. You'll have to excuse me. I'm suddenly not feeling well... at all. I've been trying to fight off a cold. I shouldn't have come."

"Irina, are you sure? You brought dinner," Robert said.

I stood up. "It's not enough for everyone."

"Robert, I thought you made reservations for the three of us at Le Chateau," Monica said.

I looked at Monica. Reservations? I suppose they would have Ile Flottante for dessert. My smile remained frozen. "Yes, I'm quite sure. Could you please get my coat? It was nice meeting you, Theo."

Robert walked me to the door. "Irina, I'll call you tomorrow." He gave me a kiss on my cheek. "Thanks for dinner."

As I walked to the elevator, a tear rolled down my cheek. I couldn't help thinking about some parallels to Swan Lake and my relationship with Robert. I thought of the prince's betrayal and poor Odette. Robert had professed his love for me in college for four years and then went off with another, Samantha to whom he also professed his love.

When I reached the lobby, the doorman smiled at me while telling a patron that the concierge would handle their request. I tried hard to not burst out crying.

* * * *

Nearing my brownstone, a block ahead of me, I saw Tricia and Alice walking. Then Alice took a running start and slid on the snow. She must have had a successful event. Tricia reached down and made a snowball, then threw it at Alice and laughed. So much for the grieving widow.

I entered the brownstone and went straight to Margarite's door.

When she opened the door I spewed out, "The jerk. He got her pregnant while we were living together."

Margarite looked on either side of me down the hall. "You'd better come in."

"Only for a few minutes. I know you are busy preparing dinner for your friend."

"Everything is finished that can be until just before we eat. She's not coming for another hour."

Margarite poured us a glass of wine and we sat down in front of her fireplace. I explained what happened.

"Samantha was pregnant when Robert and I were living together. She was my friend as well. They both betrayed me."

"That's terrible, but it was so long ago. Robert probably couldn't bring himself to tell you. Maybe that's why he didn't tell you about his son visiting."

"Another thing, we've slept together and his son never heard of me. That's how important I am to Robert."

"I told you to go slow with him."

I crossed my arms. "You never said that. Going slow isn't your style."

"Well, I should have. I totally agree. The guy is a jerk. Always was, always will be."

I could feel a vein pulsating on the side of my forehead. "Why hadn't I seen this coming? Why didn't I see it before?

Why did Jerome want this reunion? He of all people knew how traumatic it was when Robert left. I cried on his shoulders those first few months. Jerome was there to pick up the pieces."

"Men have selective memories."

Margarite's cat Gypsy came and curled up next to my feet. I reached down petting her. After a while I calmed down. I told Margarite about seeing Alice and Tricia throwing snowballs around and laughing.

"Life will be easier for Alice with Stephen gone," Margarite said.

I reached down to pet Gypsy again. She jumped on my lap. I smiled. "Good, Gypsy."

Chapter Twelve

Monday, February 23

At nine o'clock I entered the police station on West 82nd between Amsterdam and Columbus. I asked for Police Lieutenant Charles Whitney. The station house was busy, and the comings and goings were interesting to watch. Lots of police officers were about, one was giving a tour to three suited men. A homeless man and woman sat on a bench close to me. At least they looked homeless. Two women paraded past me in spiky heels, their open coats revealed flimsy, silky tops and short skirts. The way they dressed, I wondered if they were prostitutes.

I stood up when I saw a relaxed and confident Charles walking towards me. He greeted me by way of a hand shake.

"Did you find out if an autopsy was done?"

Charles took me by the crook of my arm and led me to his office. Along the way we walked past whiteboard covered walls with case notes and photos of wanted criminals taped to them. Desks with officers talking noisily on the phones were placed haphazardly around the large, open room. Officers, some in plainclothes but with their badges hanging from their necks on chains, were bringing criminals in handcuffs through the area, winding them amid the desks.

Charles offered me a seat in his office, then sat at his desk before answering my question. "Irina, not that I know of. We're usually contacted."

I glanced out his open-blind window, so intrigued by all the chaos in the bullpen.

Charles cleared his throat. "Irina, I don't know about the autopsy."

My attention went back to him. "How could that have happened? No autopsy?"

He shrugged his shoulders and leaned back in his desk chair. "Most deaths don't result in an autopsy being performed. Although if there is a suspicious death, the medical examiner can order one even without the consent of the next of kin."

"This is a suspicious death. I told the coroner in the hallway outside of Stephen's apartment just that."

Charles looked up at the ceiling.

I followed his eyes, then took the baggie, that contained Stephen's hair, out of my purse and handed it to Charles. "I took the hair samples from a navy-striped sweater that Stephen wore the day before he died. He was at my home."

Charles looked at the baggie. "Irina, you do realize that each half inch of hair relates to approximately a thirty day time segment of the sample donor?"

"I didn't know that."

He rubbed his eyebrow. "If Stephen was poisoned, resulting in his death, this hair sample isn't going to prove that."

I supposed that made sense. "But, if he had been poisoned all along and the poison built up in his system, wouldn't his hair show that?"

"Normally the district attorney would have to present a case to get approval to have certain tests run."

"Charles..."

"Okay, I can see you aren't going to let this go. Charles paused a minute and reached in his desk bringing out an official evidence bag. He transferred the hair sample. I'll be back. Wait here. I have someone who owes me a favor."

I wanted to throw my arms around his neck, but with the walls made of windows I settled for a "Thank you."

While I waited for Charles to return, I looked over the mounds of paper work on his desk, then out into the office bullpen again. I stood up and went over to the window when I saw a handcuffed criminal, a man in a bandanna, elbow his handler and tried to make a break for it. It only lasted about a second or two before three officers had him back under control.

Charles entered the room. "Okay, that's done. Have you eaten yet? I'm famished. How does brunch sound?"

I looked at my watch. "I didn't expect you to take me out for brunch, but ballet class isn't until this afternoon."

"Then it's settled. I know a great little restaurant in the West Village," he said.

As we left Charles' office, a man who Charles mentioned was the deputy chief was walking around the floor, yelling at everyone about some case or another. Charles was stopped a couple of times by officers. As he talked to them, one looked like an undercover detective, I noticed one desk officer hang up his phone, gather up a few other officers, and they ran out of the room. I imagined they headed toward the motor pool to respond to something that must have just been discussed on the phone.

Outside, Charles hailed a taxi and we made our way to the heart of the West Village. "How can you work with all of that chaos surrounding you?"

"What? Oh, in the police station? You block it out after awhile. Just as you blocked out the audience while you were up on stage concentrating only on your technique." He smiled and hooked his arm through mine.

I nodded in agreement. "I hope the results come back soon. The funeral is the end of this week. Tricia plans on

130

having Stephen cremated. Then any hope of foul play will be cast away."

"I sent your sample ASAP. They should be able to get the report soon. Let's not think about all of that for now and enjoy each other's company."

When we arrived, I realized I had passed Jardinière on foot many times, but had never been inside. The maitre d' greeted Charles by name and showed us to a table. It seemed like all of the maitre d's in Manhattan had accents. It turned out, Charles had a standing reservation. The restaurant had the elegance of old world dining and the warmth of a neighborhood cafe.

While we waited for our food to come, I ordered the Spinach and Gruyere Quiche, Charles, the Strawberries Crêpe Romanoff, Charles said, "Irina, you seem a bit distracted. How is everything going with your friend, Robert?"

I told him about Robert's son visiting and that he hadn't even mentioned me to Theo.

Charles leaned in and reached across the table, putting his hand over mine. "Robert's a fool if he's taking you for granted."

I smiled. His hand was comforting. "Thank you, Charles."

"I mean it. A *total* fool. He's not up to your caliber. *At all.*"

"You're very sweet."

He smiled, his eye contact unwavering. "I'm not being sweet, just truthful. I could tell the moment I met him."

I raised my eyebrows.

Our food arrived. He put his hand back on his lap and smiled at the server. Everything looked fresh and was presented beautifully, detail perfect.

"Irina, there's a foreign film I've been wanting to see. 'Valse Obliée.' Would you be interested in going some evening this week?"

131

Listz's Valse Obliée. I danced to Listz's Valse Obliée. It was on my last evening in Lithuania. The music was about a troubled spirit seeking consolation. How fitting the music was. I had just found out about my young lover, the KGB agent. It might have been the performance of my career. In so many ways, I lived the music.

"Irina?" Charles said, his eyes bright.

"Charles, the film sounds interesting. I'd love to see it with you."

"Friday evening? We could sneak in a quick bite to eat before the film starts."

I thought about Stephen's funeral being that day. "It's a date. I look forward to it."

* * * *

After I came back from what ended up being a very long brunch, I started getting ready for ballet class. I smiled, thinking about the children's excitement and progress they had made. It was a labor of love being a role model for these young dancers. I thought it important that they saw, at their young age, ballet as enjoyment.

When I left to go to class, walking down the brownstone steps, I heard someone calling out my name. It was Michel. I waited for him. He walked with me to the ballet studio talking about our weekends. He had attended a lecture at The Met on the Arts of the Islamic World. It was given in French. He especially enjoyed that. When we arrived at the studio, we made another date for coffee on Wednesday.

I was never more happy than when dancing. The children eager to please, followed my lead as they learned new moves to be woven into the music for our recital. As always, I had to hold back from smiling large when little Ivy fell going from one movement to another, each time Molly helping her up. By the end of class, everything seemed to be coming together. For only having a few sessions with the new music, I was amazed at how well the children were doing and how enthusiastic they remained.

When the last of the children had been collected, Jerome and I talked sitting at the piano.

He played a few notes than stopped. "Irina, the report about the plants came back."

"Really? Were they poisonous?"

He shook his head. "The plants were nothing out of the ordinary. They were coriander."

I looked from the keys to Jerome. "Shoot! That's what Alice mentioned they were."

Jerome continued. "They were infested with bugs, probably why they were thrown out."

I played a few lower notes. "Looks like that's a dead-end." I told Jerome about Stephen's nootropics and about my meeting Theo.

"Irina, I had no idea that Robert and Samantha had Theo that year. I didn't even converse with Robert for a few years, because of his leaving you so abruptly." Jerome looked over at me. "I was with you. Totally there for you. When we finally did start corresponding, they already had Theo." He played a familiar riff.

I shook my head. "I must say it was a shock learning about him."

Jerome stopped playing and looked at me. "If Monica is like an aunt to Theo and his brother, that would explain why she was there. She did put her hand on Theo's knee, not Robert's."

I quivered. "I thought it was a bit awkward when she did that."

"Irina, I understand you being angry to learn Samantha got pregnant when you were living with Robert. But that was so long ago. We were young, stupid, and confused. Everyone made mistakes. Trust me, Robert isn't like that any longer."

Jerome started playing and singing 'Young Americans' by David Bowie. The first verse was about a young man seducing a young woman and her taking his ring and his babies.

In a way, what happened to me, the affair with Vytautas, getting pregnant, happened to Samantha. The big difference was that I didn't have an affair with my friend's lover. I hadn't been in a relationship with anyone when the affair occurred. And I didn't cheat on anyone as Robert had. Samantha might have instigated the affair, but Robert followed through. Robert could have thwarted her advances if that's what actually happened. They were both to blame. I started to get up from the bench. I had enough with Jerome's symbolism.

Jerome stopped playing. "Okay, Irina. It sounds to me like you're more upset about Theo not knowing who you were, rather than Robert not telling you he was visiting. Your feelings were hurt."

I kissed Jerome on his forehead and put my coat on. "Lock up on your way out."

"By the way, how did you get into Stephen's apartment to find the drugs?"

"Goodbye, Jerome."

As I went out the door I heard Jerome resuming the song.

* * * *

Walking back home, I thought about Alice saying the same thing about the plants that the tests revealed. But why did she go through the trouble of throwing them in the neighbor's garbage? That seemed kind of shifty and didn't make much sense to me. Perhaps I should have taken samples of food? Then again, Stephen was taking all of those brain-boosting drugs. An autopsy needed to be done to figure all of this out and stop all of the guessing. Time was running out! As I approached the brownstone, I saw the garbage truck pulling away. Too late for any further garbage picking.

As I started up the cement steps, I heard my name called out. Tricia had just gotten out of a taxi.

I waited for her. When she reached me I asked, "How are you holding up?" It looked like years had been added to her face just in the last several days.

"I decided to go into work today. It keeps my mind off of Stephen. I wanted to tell you we moved Stephen's funeral up to Wednesday afternoon. His sister arrived early and since it will be a small affair, I was able to get the same restaurant for the funeral luncheon.

Oh, no! "When will Stephen be cremated?"

She gave me an odd look, her forehead wrinkling. "Wednesday morning."

Wednesday? In two days. I unlocked the door to our building.

"I hope you and Margarite can make it to the funeral."

"Of course we'll be there. I'll tell Margarite. She'll need to take off of work. But have you contacted the police or the medical examiner to get their permission for Stephen's body to be delivered to the funeral home? How do you know everything will be ready by Wednesday?"

"Police? Medical Examiner? Irina, what are you talking about? The funeral home takes care of all of that."

"Tricia, I brought this up before. Don't you want to find out what Stephen died from? With an autopsy?" I knew I was being pushy, but time was running out.

She wasn't upset this time with the mention of one. "Of course not. He had the flu. There have been many deaths from the flu this year, all over the country. I don't need an autopsy to tell me that. And don't bring this up again with Alice, she'll flip out."

"It seemed worse than the flu and occurred for a long time."

Tricia made an evasive gesture and shook her head.

Was this Tricia's way of dealing with Stephen's death, a kind of defense mechanism, ignoring the fact that something suspicious could have come into play in his death?

135

We walked down the hall to her apartment. "You may as well know, we're thinking about putting the apartment up for sale. Too much of Stephen here. Alice reminded me over the weekend, it was Stephen's dream to live in the brownstone not mine."

"Do you think it's wise to make hasty decisions at this time? You might feel differently about that in a few weeks. It isn't easy to get a great apartment like yours."

Her eyes narrowed. "I'm getting tired of everyone telling me what to do."

I didn't say anything. Looking at Tricia, she seemed to have aged in one short week. The sparkle in her eyes was replaced by shadows under them. Her hair had lost its shine. She had a pinched expression.

"I'm sorry, Irina. Alice is constantly telling me about what I need to do."

"Stand up for yourself. What kind of things? Would you like to come in for coffee and talk about it?"

"Thank you, I can't. Alice wants me to look through the rental ads. By the way, I'd like my key back to the apartment."

"Of course. I'll go get it. You can come in and wait if you'd like."

Tricia stayed out in the hall. I gave her back the key, she thanked me, and went into her apartment. When she closed the door, I heard a number of locks sound. I saw the peephole darkened. Was she looking?

Had she known someone was in her apartment looking around? Did she suspect it was me?

That evening I stayed in and I looked up the names of the drugs I had written down from Stephen's bottles. All were nootropics. It looked like he was heavily into them, which again invoked many questions. The main one, had Stephen caused his own death from an overdose? Without an autopsy being done, the mystery would die with his cremation.

I went into the kitchen and poured a glass of cabernet. I never received a call from Robert to go with him and Theo to attend the play. I wasn't sure I would have accepted, had he called. Perhaps he changed his mind about seeing one. I put on a jazz album and picked up my mystery book.

Chapter Thirteen

Tuesday, February 24

That morning Charles stopped in on his way to the office, not wanting to discuss the case with me again at the police station. We sat in the kitchen while waiting for the coffee to finish.

"Ethylene glycol was found in Stephen's system."

Coffee ready, I poured him a cup. "Ethylene glycol? What's that?"

"Antifreeze."

I wrinkled my brow. "Antifreeze? What on earth?" All was quiet for a few seconds. Stephen was poisoned with antifreeze? "That's unreal. Who could have gotten Stephen to drink antifreeze?" I said to myself out loud.

Charles shook his head.

"Thank goodness there was an autopsy after all. When was it done?"

"Yesterday evening. Although the medical examiner did collect physical evidence after the death. Blood, urine, stomach contents, liver, bile, that sort of thing."

"Now something can be done about his death," I said, as I sat down at the kitchen table. Poor Stephen. "Will the evidence still be valid?"

"Yes. The medical examiner stored everything properly to ensure the integrity. He had a hunch it might be needed later for testing."

A big hunch. I told him to do an autopsy. "I bet he had collected the body fluids because Stephen was so young."

"Besides severe acidosis, he said he found something he called oxalate crystals in the kidney."

"Oxalate what?"

"In the kidneys. That points to ethylene glycol poisoning."

Charles took a sip of his coffee then smiled. "Hmm. Nice and strong. Just how I like it." He put his cup down. "I talked with him, he mentioned about a 'nosy parker' being in the apartment hallway that evening."

I hesitated, then got up. Charles knew that person was me. Thank goodness I said something to the medical examiner that evening. Taking three plates out of the cupboard, I put a couple of blueberry muffins on one, then placed napkins and the plates on the table. "Perhaps it was a good thing there was a 'nosy parker' in the hallway."

Charles reached for a muffin and took a generous bite from it. "Excellent home baked muffins and the best coffee. Irina, I may be showing up at your door every morning. What a treat."

"You'd be welcome." Back in my chair, I said, "Then it *was* murder."

"Or Stephen killed himself."

I sighed and shook my head. "No, Charles. No!" I couldn't believe how much I raised my voice. Bringing it back down a level, I said, "Stephen told me he was trying for a new position, a promotion, even on his last day alive when he was so sick. He never would have killed himself."

He looked at me shrewdly and took another bite of the muffin. "Maybe he didn't get the promotion. Have you considered that?"

I fidgeted with my coffee cup. "Never. Not Stephen. That wouldn't have been the end of the world for him. Besides people don't kill themselves when they don't get promotions." After I said all of this, I thought about the nootropics we had found that Stephen had been using. He must have been desperate to use all those mind enhancing drugs. "And death by antifreeze?" I shook my head. "I don't believe that at all!"

Charles wiped his mouth. "Irina, this is enough evidence to start an investigation. That's what you wanted."

"You're right." I put the coffee cup down. "Good. I'll see what I can do to—"

Clearing his throat, he said, "Irina, it's a police matter. You've done your part. We'll be asking the questions from now on. This might have dropped off the radar if you hadn't been suspicious and brought us the hair samples to spur on the investigation." He held my gaze. "Why am I getting the impression I'm not really reaching you?"

"The hair samples helped?"

His face reddened. "Well, no, not really. But they did trigger the investigation." He hesitated and said quietly, "Calling in the favor."

Oh right. The favor. It must have been a BIG favor.

"Irina, you got the results you wanted. Now, please, let the police take over. As you said, there could be a murderer out there." He finished his coffee.

"Sure." Tricia and Alice didn't have a car to use antifreeze. I suppose they could have bought some.

After putting his coffee cup down he said, "One last thing. The stomach contents were reduced to a liquid pulp, but traces of two flowers, delphiniums and larkspur were found."

"Flowers? How odd."

"They're toxic, but there weren't enough to kill. Still, nothing a person would ordinarily ingest."

"Larkspur and delphiniums are quite similar. They must have been concealed in his food. I knew I was right about Tricia and Alice."

He stood up. "Now don't jump to conclusions. And don't tell anyone what we've just discussed."

"So there were two different poisons involved," I said, as I went and got Charles' coat out of the front closet. "What would explain the two poisons? If one didn't work, the other would? Seems like the antifreeze would have been enough to do the job. Why mess with the flowers? Those would have been hard to disguise in food. I suppose they might have looked like spices."

As he put his coat on, his voice wavered, "If he didn't kill himself, someone definitely wanted him dead. How would you have characterized Stephen?"

"He was a really lovely guy. Personable. He and his wife were great neighbors, that is until Tricia's sister Alice moved in with them. Then they started having problems. What about Stephen's funeral? It's tomorrow."

"Isn't going to happen. Irina, I'll call you later to set up a time and place for Friday. Looking forward to our date." He kissed me on my cheek and left.

I smiled closing the door. I hadn't been out with Charles for a while. We always had an enjoyable time together. I went back into the kitchen and put the dishes into the dishwasher, going over what we just discussed. I couldn't wait until Margarite got home from school to tell her about the antifreeze and the flowers in Stephen's stomach contents. This was proof that Stephen was definitely murdered no matter what Charles thought.

About five minutes later there was a knock on the door. Thinking Charles had forgotten to tell me something, I hurried to the door and opened it to find Tricia standing there weeping.

"I came over to tell you that Stephen's funeral isn't going to be tomorrow." Tears streamed down her cheeks. She wiped her eyes with her hand. "I received a phone call from the police. They think Stephen was murdered. Can you believe it? Who would have murdered Stephen? Everyone loved him."

She was crying so hard I could barely understand her. If I hadn't just had the conversation with Charles, I wouldn't have been able to make out what she was saying. I was glad she didn't come over when Charles was here. "Why don't you come in? I have coffee made."

"I can't stay. There are so many people to contact. Perhaps, just for a minute. I don't even know when they will release Stephen's body." She started sobbing harder.

I invited her to sit on the sofa. "Murdered? What makes the medical examiner think Stephen was murdered?" I kept secret what I knew.

She took a tissue out of her pants pocket and wiped her eyes, then started crying again. "An autopsy was performed and poison was found."

I put my arm around her shoulders. "Poison? How terrible. I'm so sorry. Were you told the type of poison?"

She shrugged. "Who could have...how?"

I knew now might not be a good time, but it wasn't often I had Tricia alone. "Stephen had told me he was vying for a new position at work. Were there many contenders?"

"A few. One was a friend and business associate. It was a game with them, always competing against each other."

"Alex Rankin?"

She turned and faced me on the sofa. My arm dropped. She gave me an incredulous stare. "Why, yes. Of course, I believe I've mentioned him to you before. He's a friend of ours. We had gone out with him and his girlfriends a number of times."

It didn't sound to me like Stephen and Alex were great friends. Did Tricia enjoy his company more than Stephen?

"Stephen introduced me to Alex in the hallway when leaving on his trip. It was the time when I helped Stephen put one of your health shakes into his overnight case. His hands were trembling so bad. He told me you usually made those for him to take to work. The shakes." I gave a questioning look.

Her face reddened. A tightness appeared in her expression. "So? You don't think... We were trying to help Stephen."

We? So it wasn't just her concoctions. Tricia seemed so defensive with a simple statement. Did she have a guilty conscience, that she would interpret what I was saying that way? I *was* getting at that, but definitely in a roundabout way.

She stood up. "I loved my husband."

I stood up as well. "Tricia, I know you did. But what about Alice? Did she like him?"

"Of course. Alice and I, we were both concerned about Stephen's health. Alice even grew some of the medicinal herbs for his shakes. You saw them."

Was Tricia kept in the dark about the poisonous flowers? Or did she in fact know?

Her eyes narrowed. "It wasn't us who poisoned him if that's what your getting at." Then she mumbled, "Alice said any food was probably already absorbed into his body."

Absorbed into his body? Or so she wished. What a slip of the tongue! Was she so upset to not even have noticed what she just said? Or was she still innocently assuming they were health shakes. And Alice, she would know that kind of information being a murder mystery author. I'm sure she knew many methods of murder. "Tricia, I'm not making accusations." Really I was. I decided to change the subject or they would be bringing me health shakes. "I'm sorry. I'll let Margarite know about Stephen's funeral."

After Tricia left, I had another cup of coffee and thought more about what Charles had told me. I remembered seeing dried flowers in Tricia and Alice's trash can when I was looking for the plants. But were they larkspur or delphiniums? I couldn't remember. If only I had put those also in my bag.

I never got around to canceling my meeting with Michel for tomorrow because of the funeral. Now there wouldn't be a problem meeting with him. I decided to give him a call to get more details as to our meeting time and place.

"Michel, there's a fabulous bakery in the Village that has to die for cakes, even some European varieties," I said.

"That's close to Chelsea Market? I haven't been there yet."

"It's a bit of a hike, but close enough. We could walk there after coffee. It would be fun."

"Sounds like a great day. I don't have any classes after eleven o'clock. Is that a good time for you? I could come by your place."

* * * *

Later in the afternoon, just as I was ready to see if Margarite was home from school to tell her about the funeral being cancelled, my door buzzed. I looked down the hall and saw Robert standing outside the front door smiling. He waved. I walked over and opened the door.

"Irina, thought I'd take a chance and come over rather than just call. I'm glad you're home. Can I come in?"

That worked well when I did the same at your apartment. "Hello Robert. Where's Theo?"

He bit at his lips a little. "He was only here for the weekend. I'm sorry we never made it to the play." He averted his eyes. "He said he thought you were a very nice person."

"Had he ever heard of me before his visit?"

I started walking down towards my door.

Robert cleared his throat. "To be truthful, Irina, not really. I didn't know how the kids would take it, getting involved so soon after Samantha's death."

My eyes went wide. I opened the door to my apartment, then closed it again, remaining in the hall. I turned around

144

facing Robert. Really, a forty year old man? "Robert, what did you want to see me about?"

He leaned in and kissed me softly on my lips. "How would you like to spend the day together tomorrow? I thought perhaps we could still go to that play. The reviews are great. Or to another art museum, if you'd rather."

For a second I lost track of time, my surroundings, everything. Then I snapped out of it. I shook my head. "I'm sorry, Robert, I have plans."

"With... Margarite?"

"No. She teaches."

"Of course."

"With Michel, my new young friend. He's a few years younger than Theo and is new to the neighborhood. You remember, I've talked about him. He's French." I then smiled thinking about Michel. "Remember, he and I had coffee the day we met up with Monica and Todd."

"Couldn't you change those plans to another day?"

It would be great to spend the day with Robert. "No. I wouldn't do that."

"Why again is he so interested in you?"

I laughed. "Could be he thinks I'm a fascinating person."

He shrugged. A shrug I didn't like. "What about dinner this evening? You haven't spent much time at my place. I could make a romantic dinner, candlelight, music, wine. Give you the grand tour." He smiled. "Perhaps you'd like to bring an overnight bag."

I needed to rethink our relationship. "I'm sorry. I have plans with Margarite for dinner." I lied. "Perhaps another time."

Robert's lips parted slightly. He leaned in. "Dinner on Friday then?"

"Robert, you're going to find this hard to believe, but—"

Robert's face began to redden. "You have plans Friday evening."

I fidgeted with my hands. "This is a busy week."

He said in a rushed voice, his face going from a hurt look to a more angry one, "You're right. I do find that hard to believe. If you are ever able to fit me into your busy schedule, you know where you can find me."

As he started for the outside door, Margarite came in carrying a bag of groceries and her school bag. I followed Robert to the door. When Margarite looked at me I raised my eyebrows and widened my eyes. "Oh, Margarite, I was wondering if you'd like we could have a glass of wine at my apartment before we go out for dinner tonight."

Margarite looked between me and Robert. Robert looked at her grocery bag.

"Okay. That sounds perfect. What time again did we decide on?"

She was good at improvisation.

As the three of us stood at the opened front door, Alice came through with Alex Rankin in tow, without so much as a smile or a hello. My mouth fell open as they passed on their way to Tricia's apartment.

After Robert left, Margarite took me by the crook of my arm and said, "Okay, so what was that all about with Robert?"

"Never mind about Robert. That was Alex Rankin, Stephen's co-worker, who just came in with Alice. I wonder what that's about?"

I followed Margarite into her apartment where she put away the groceries and then we went back to mine where we did have a glass of wine. I told her about the autopsy, Tricia and the funeral, Alice, Michel, and Robert and Charles. And Alex Rankin.

We ordered in Chinese food.

Chapter Fourteen

Wednesday, February 25

As we rode the subway to Greenwich Village, I smiled, reminiscing about dancing to Listz's Valse Obliée on my last evening in Lithuania. Michel had inquired about my performances there. I mentioned I was going to see the movie. Next our discussion turned to what we enjoyed most about Manhattan: Central Park, The Met, Lincoln Center, the Theatres. I glanced down at the small brown paper package he held on his lap. What was in there?

We got off the subway at Union Square on 14th Street. The atmosphere was electric at Union Square's Greenmarket, a popular New York City's farmers' market. Michel and I had a cup of hot apple cider to warm ourselves as we checked out some of the vendors. The number of vendors shrunk to half during the winter months, making it easier and more pleasurable to get around. Root vegetables dominated most of the produce selections. Deciding it was a bit cold, we headed to A Baker's Daughter, Michel clutching the paper bag close to his body.

A Baker's Daughter was situated between a used bookstore and a vintage jewelry shop on Broadway between 13th and 14th Street. We stopped for a quick glance at the jewelry in the window. Entering the cozy restaurant, the aroma of the freshly baked goods greeted us along with the proprietor. We took a table by the window and looked at the menu. Michel ordered a piece of Black Forest cake. I could never resist my favorite dessert and chose the flourless chocolate cake.

"You have my curiosity piqued. What's in the bag?"

He smiled. "A surprise, Irina." He then changed the subject. "Usually when I tell people I'm from France, they start telling me about how much they love Paris."

"It *is* a romantic city."

Michel cocked his head to one side. "Was it romantic for you?"

Our cake arrived along with the coffee. Taken aback by his question, I took a forkful of cake, smiled, and said, "No. I can't say my memories about Paris were romantic."

"I was born in France, but I'm not French."

I put my fork down. "Really?"

"Yes. I was adopted by a French couple from an orphanage there."

I took a sip of my coffee. My heart started to pound. "Oh," I said quietly and shifted in my chair.

He looked deeply into my eyes. "Château de Chevrier."

I let out a small gasp and put my hand to my throat. "Château de Chevrier. Oh Michel."

"My ancestry is Russian and American," he continued.

If this were an Agatha Christie novel, I might ask for DNA testing, but I looked deep into Michel's eyes. I saw my mother's. I smiled. "I have a feeling you may also be Lithuanian."

Michel took in a deep breath. "Then you've guessed. Irina, your name was on my birth certificate. I am your..."

He opened the paper bag and carefully removed what looked like a well-loved teddy bear. He looked at it tenderly and said, "This teddy bear was left with me by..."

Tears filled my eyes. "Oh, Michel, I remember. I wanted to leave you something, something I had touched. Something to connect me to you and you to..." Michel reached into his pocket and handed me his immaculate white handkerchief. I wiped my eyes. "Thank you." I put his handkerchief on my lap.

He reached for my hand, gently holding the teddy bear with his other. His hand was trembling. "I've always kept it with me."

"You are so handsome and grownup." I laughed. "Of course, you're grownup."

He laughed.

"Oh, Michel, I am so sorry." I picked up his handkerchief and wiped my eyes again. "I was young and I wanted a good life for you. A life I couldn't give you then."

"I was adopted by loving parents, but I wanted to meet you. I'm pleased to see my birth mother is such a kind woman." His eyes sparkled.

"I kept praying that you would be adopted by a kind family. I thought about you often. Many times I wanted to find you. I did inquire and was told you were adopted a few weeks after you came to the orphanage. I was happy about that, but that was all I was told. No names, no idea where you were. Everything was so secretive." I paused for a few moments, my lips starting to tremble. "I always hoped you wouldn't hate me." Tears started forming in my eyes again. I wiped my eyes. "I came to think I didn't have the right to interfere with your new life."

Michel put the teddy bear down and held out his hand to me again. "Of course I don't hate you. I could never hate you."

I smiled. "I can see you were well loved. How did you find me?"

A number of years ago I searched through records before the orphanage was demolished. It was written down you were with an American ballet company."

"I wonder how they knew I was with the ballet company."

He shrugged his shoulders. "Perhaps someone recognized you."

I smiled. "I'm glad they did."

"My parents were both sickly. I waited before trying to find you. After my parents were gone, I applied for the position at Columbia and almost didn't get it. I looked up your name and saw you had the ballet school.

"I'm sorry about your parents. I'm happy they were kind and loving and gave you a good home."

His eyes welled up with tears. Tears rolled down my cheeks. "So it wasn't a coincidence I kept bumping into you."

Michel laughed, then sniffed his nose. "No."

I laughed, then wiped my eyes again.

"I wanted to learn more about you first."

"I often imagined who you were and what you were like. I couldn't be happier, Michel."

He smiled. "Tell me about my father. I don't know anything about him."

I squinted looking at him. "Now that I know you are his son, I do see a resemblance to him."

"Was he also kind, like you?" Michel asked with a questioning smile.

I hesitated. I could feel my heart race. What would I tell Michel? I didn't want to speak unkindly. But I didn't want to lie. And I needed to say something.

"Your father was a student. He seemed kind."

Michel's forehead wrinkled. "Seemed kind?"

I spoke about his Vytautas' art and book interests, the political climate of Lithuania at the time, and was honest in what I said. "You were conceived out of love. My love for your father was real and true. At the time, I felt your father's love was the same for me. He never knew about you." I told Michel about learning he might have been a KGB agent.

He looked at me intently. "And what if he wasn't KGB?"

I looked down, and picked up my fork. "Then I would have been foolish and might have made the biggest mistake of my life." I put my fork back down and looked at Michel. "In my heart I don't believe I was mistaken. Later my family learned of the atrocities on the Lithuanian people by the KGB. I was glad I hadn't told him."

I glanced for a second out of the window trying to collect my thoughts, then turned to Michel. "And now... "I quickly did a double-take and looked back outside, my posture stiffening. Across the street, Robert and Monica walked arm in arm unhurriedly.

"And now...?" Michel asked looking at me and then out the window.

My heart started pounding again. I turned away from the window, barely believing what I saw. "I'd love to spend more time with you if you will allow me to. We have so much catching up to do."

"I'd love that also, Irina."

I smiled. I was so happy. We finished our cake and coffee. I didn't want thoughts of Robert and Monica interfering in this most important moment of learning that Michel was my son. My son! I pinched myself a couple of times under the table to make sure this wasn't a dream. I had dreamed often of one day being with my son.

We walked towards Chelsea Market. On the way I slipped on a patch of ice. Michel grabbed for me trying to prevent my fall. Instead we both fell down and started laughing. Once again vertical, Michel took me by the crook of my arm as we proceeded on.

Perhaps this was all it was with Robert and Monica. One of them slipped and they steadied themselves. I wanted to give Robert the benefit of the doubt. Besides, Monica had a partner of forty years. You don't just throw forty years away.

Wandering through the various shops at Chelsea Market, we stopped at one vendor and looked at the array of beautiful

151

teas and spices. I choose cardamon pods for tea and a tin of chai black tea. Michel wanted me to help him choose a cast iron teapot to give for a gift. They had a beautiful selection of teapots. It was hard to select only one.

After finally deciding, I told Michel about Stephen and that foul play was involved.

When they packaged up our purchases, Michel said, "Irina, I knew Stephen. I had seen him coming from your building."

We left the spice and tea store and continued walking. For a second I thought back to when Margarite had mentioned it was a bit of a coincidence that both Robert and Michel showed up around the same time that Stephen died. "How did you know him?"

"He played racquetball at my club. And I know his partner as well."

My eyes opened wide. "Alex Rankin?"

"Right. Talk about competitive. You couldn't help but hear the two of them in the locker room. Alex was the more intense of the two. Quite the braggart."

"Competitive about work?"

"Everything from what I heard. Their accomplishments at work, skill at racquetball, the latest technology they owned. Even with all of his bragging, I always felt Alex had a great deal of self-doubt. A fragile self-esteem if you will, which depended on his last accomplishment or whom he could impress."

"It doesn't sounds like he had a healthy sense of competition or much respect for Stephen."

"I agree. And I've watched them play. Alex was ruthless."

I raised my eyebrows. "What's the name of the club?"

"New York Racquet Club in Midtown."

While we looked through a bookstore, my mind was on Alex. After what Michel said, I wondered if he felt the need to

152

eliminate his competition? Was this a motive for murder? What about Alice? She was with him. And Tricia? Poor Stephen. Did he ever have a chance? Was I grasping at straws? Who profited the most by Stephen's death? "I need to learn more about Alex." Saying this, I suddenly felt guilty. I just found out about Michel being my son. This time should be about Michel not Alex. I should be enjoying Michel's company and not thinking or talking about Alex.

"I can help you to find out more. Perhaps even the truth."

"Michel, are you sure? I hate to burden you or involve you with all of this. We have so many other things to talk about. So much to learn about each other."

Michel nodded. "Irina, are you free for dinner tomorrow evening? We could plan a strategy."

"I would love to have you come to my home for dinner. We could plan there?"

On the way home, I thought, my son, my dear son and I were going to have dinner together at my home. Never in my wildest dreams had I imaged this.

* * * *

Later that afternoon I called Jerome saying I wanted to discuss the music for Friday's class. What I really wanted was to get some reassurance from him regarding Robert. He had always been my anchor, the person I went to for comfort when it came to Robert. But first I told him about Michel. He had noticed the resemblance before I did.

"A son? My God, Irina, what other secrets have you been holding back on? Do you have other children?"

After convincing him I didn't have other children, I told him about seeing Robert and Monica.

"He did ask you to spend the day with him and several evenings. He probably wanted to get out of his apartment. Do you think you might be just a bit too hard on him? He hurt your feelings regarding Theo, but has he done anything else to warrant throwing away your relationship? It's not like he's having an affair with Monica. Relax. They were walking down the street together."

Jerome seemed totally oblivious about Robert. I couldn't quite understand his attitude. Changing the subject, I mentioned the autopsy results.

He clicked his tongue. "Irina, it doesn't make sense that the wife and sister would poison him with flowers and also antifreeze. Why bother with the former?"

"I had exactly the same thought," I said.

"I bet they aren't the culprits. Alice's strange behavior isn't necessarily a sign of guilt. She might just be a nasty person."

"But there was Tricia's slip of Alice's comment on the absorption of stomach contents."

"True."

* * * *

After I hung up, I went into the kitchen and gathered my thoughts over a cup of coffee. I decided to make a list of everything I knew about Stephen's death.

1. Tricia and Alice made daily "health" shakes for Stephen. Were they more like "death" shakes? Were they that evil?

2. Stephen appeared better after he was away from home for a few days. Then he became sick again after his return. Too much of a coincidence?

3. Alice wasn't fond of Stephen. She was telling Tricia to do things Tricia didn't want to do. What were those things?

4. I saw divorce papers in Stephen's desk. Was there a prenuptial agreement? Might Tricia not have benefited as well with a divorce? Still, to kill someone?

5. Stephen was up against a competitive partner for a promotion at work and a more prestigious job. There was an overzealous partner who seemed to have some kind of a relationship with Stephen's wife and sister-in-law.

6. Stephen died from antifreeze poisoning. But poisonous flowers were also found in his system. Why two methods of poison when one should have done the job?

7. What was Celeste doing at Tricia's door? Was she somehow involved in Stephen's murder? Was she there to retrieve some incriminating evidence?

8. <u>Suspects</u> - I underlined the word suspects. Tricia? Alice? Tricia and Alice? Alex? Stephen? Charles had mentioned suicide. I didn't believe that. Who else? Celeste? Again, who profited the most from Stephen's death? Someone I hadn't met? Or knew?

<u>Plan</u> – Rule out Alex. Would I get anymore information from Alice or Tricia about him? Learn more about Celeste. Find out the connection between Alice and Alex. Brainstorm with Michel tomorrow evening as to our plan of action. Keep up with Charles and the police investigation.

Chapter Fifteen

Thursday, February 26

That morning, I knocked on Tricia's door after I saw Alice leaving the building. Even though I thought I wouldn't get anything else from Tricia regarding Alex, I decided to try and "squeeze blood from a turnip." I wasn't one to give up.

"I still can't believe they won't release Stephen's body. I called this morning again," Tricia exclaimed when she opened the door.

"I'm sorry, Tricia."

Tricia closed the door and motioned to the sofa. We both sat down. "How am I supposed to get a funeral planned and Stephen's sister is already here?"

"Something has been bothering me," I said knowing I had already brought up this subject to her. "Stephen had mentioned he was up for a promotion. Do you know if anyone got the promotion?"

"Promotion? What does that matter now? And why do you even want to know all of this or even care?"

I didn't respond.

"I'm sorry, Irina. I'm not myself. It's so upsetting, waiting for the funeral." She looked at her watch. "Alex is the new Senior Design Manager. Remember I mentioned he and

Stephen were always in competition. Well, he won. Alice mentioned it yesterday."

Alex had benefited from Stephen's death. "I see. Are Alice and Alex becoming an item? I saw them together."

"Not sure if I'd call it dating. But they have gone out lately." While Tricia was talking I heard the door knob turn. I had a more important question to ask so I stood up and said, "By the way, do you have any antifreeze?"

Her mouth fell open. "Antifreeze?"

I glanced towards the door. "I have a friend whose car won't start. Thought perhaps Stephen would have some."

She shook her head, her forehead wrinkling."We don't have a car. I can't help you with that. Sorry."

Alice opened the door. I greeted her as I left the apartment and heard her say, "I forgot my writing notes. What did Irina want?"

On the way back to my apartment I saw Celeste come through the front door carrying a couple of large bags. She went up the stairs to the second floor. I decided now was as good of time as any to talk to her and learn more about her.

When I knocked on her door, she answered it still wearing her coat. She closed the door behind her. "Hello, Irina. Can I help you with something?"

"I noticed you coming into the building and thought perhaps we could chat a little, catch up. We don't see each other that often."

"I'm sorry. I'd invite you in, but my apartment is quite messy. I'd be too embarrassed."

It was silly standing out in the hall chatting so I said, "Perhaps another time. Terrible about Stephen's death. Did you know him well?"

"Not really. Just the occasional 'Hello. How are you?' I've only lived in the building for less than a year. You really are the only one I talk to here." She hesitated, then added,

"Besides Tricia and Alice on a rare occasion. I'm not even sure of the names of the people who live down the hall."

Well, that went no where. I went back to my apartment and gathered the grant application forms for SAFE, Inc. Tomorrow was my morning to volunteer at the Women and Children's Shelter. With Michel coming this evening, I wanted to make sure I'd have everything ready for tomorrow. I didn't know how late the evening would go. My mind went back to Celeste. I believed that Celeste didn't know Stephen and Tricia all that well, since she didn't even know the names of her immediate neighbors. We should have "Get To Know Your Neighbors" gatherings in this building. I finished packing up my tote for tomorrow, and thought, but then what was she doing knocking on their door?

* * * *

Early afternoon I shopped at the Whole Earth grocery store to get everything necessary for dinner with *my son*. I wanted the evening to be perfect and decided to make a spinach and prosciutto lasagna. I picked up fresh spinach, prosciutto, a variety of cheeses and a wonderful loaf of crusty bread to go with it. I'd also make a green salad and had a special wine from the Burgundy region of France at home that would pair perfectly with the lasagna.

On the way home I stopped at the neighborhood Korean market, Hana Asian Market, and looked through their bouquets of flowers for the dining room table. I was surprised, even shocked when I saw many of the bouquets contained branches of larkspur and delphiniums. After choosing one, I returned home and put everything away in its place.

Arranging the flowers in a cut glass vase I bought in Poland while on tour, I thought about how incredibly easy it would have been to obtain the flowers that Stephen had ingested. There was a source just blocks from here. Tricia had told me that's where they bought their flowers. Probably, as I had previously thought, the murderer or murderers were impatient. The flowers took too long. Who was I kidding? The only people who could have put the flowers in Stephen's food were Tricia and Alice. Why weren't the police coming up with that scenario?

Next on the agenda was the antifreeze. I looked up antifreeze on the internet and found out it had a sweet taste which made it relatively inconspicuous and could easily be mixed into a drink. In an alcoholic drink or energy drink, it wouldn't be noticed. With the first murder attempt thwarted, was Stephen given the antifreeze from the same murderers or someone else or was it a team effort.

At that moment a scary thought crossed my mind. When I asked Tricia if they had any antifreeze, and they were in fact the murderers that had laced Stephen's drinks with the substance, she would know I was on to them. And of course she would have denied having any. My stomach started to churn. What might they do if they thought I suspected? Make me a special smoothie? I would have to be more careful going forward.

Shaking my head, I decided to try and erase these thoughts from my mind. That scenario of their giving Stephen the antifreeze was a huge assumption anyway. I only wanted to think of this evening, about my son coming to dinner. My eyes teared up, drinking in the moment when I would greet my son and welcome him into my home.

I started preparing the lasagna so the dish could blend together for a few hours and then set the table in the dining room. I did as many preparations ahead of time as I could, so I would be able to spend more time with Michel and not be in the kitchen.

After dressing, it took a while to figure out an outfit a person would wear when welcoming their son into their home for the first time, I started doing last minute preps in the kitchen. When the doorbell rang, I glanced at my watch. Seven o'clock. Right on time.

"Hello Irina." Michel's smile lit up his face. He held a gift wrapped package and a bouquet of flowers. "These are for you."

For a split second I thought of Stephen. He said the same thing. Then feeling overwhelmed in a good way, I said, "The flowers are lovely. Thank you so much. Please, come in." I put the gift wrapped box on the entry table and held the flowers. Immediately I noticed the delphiniums in this bouquet as well. We hugged. "Welcome, Michel. I can't tell you how happy I am that you are here." I took his coat and smiled when I saw that he wore a crisp dress shirt and tie. Perhaps he had also lingered over what to wear as well. I had chosen a black pencil shirt, burgundy sweater, and scarf.

Returning, I led him into the kitchen where I arranged his flowers into a second cut glass vase, not as nice as the first, while we talked. I could tell we were both a little nervous. "I'll put these on the dining room table. There's a bottle of wine on the counter. Would you mind pouring us a glass?"

I quickly took the flowers I had just bought off the table and replaced them with Michel's and put mine on a side table in the living room. I picked up the wrapped gift from the entry table and placed it on the coffee table, then returned to the kitchen. "So many gifts, you shouldn't have."

After putting the lasagna in the oven, I suggested taking our drinks into the living room.

"What a beautiful home you have, Irina. It's so large. I'm in a studio over on West 80th."

"Thank you. It was my parents, your grandparents' home."

Michel looked at some original art work on the walls then went over to the table where I had put my flowers and picked up a photograph.

I watched him as he studied the photo. "Those were your grandparents."

"What a great picture." Michel put it down and picked up another photograph. He smiled. "I wish I had known them."

160

"They were wonderful people. Your grandfather was quite the storyteller. Friends would come around on a Sunday afternoons just to listen to him."

"And my grandmother, the ballerina. How beautiful she was. I love seeing these old photographs."

"I was blessed to have such devoted parents." As soon as I said that, I felt uncomfortable. I looked down thinking about how I had never been a parent to Michel.

Michel smiled. "Irina, all of these pictures tell of a beautiful life. I'm so happy I found you."

I gave him a kiss on his cheek. "I am also."

I took out a book of old photographs of my family in Lithuania to show Michel. We sat on the sofa. We each took a sip of our wine.

I put my glass down. "This is one of my favorites at my father's parents' sitting around a long covered table outside on their land."

"Look at all of the various foods and bottles of wine on the table."

"My mother told me that if you refused a food or drink that was offered, it would be thought of as an insult. She said she had too much to eat and drink that day, but didn't want to be rude."

Michel laughed. "They had a lovely flower garden."

"My father brought back soil from his parents' land. I still have it in a decorative box I bought in Lithuania when I was there. I motioned to it on the table with the photos."

"You should have this photograph framed and be with the others on the table."

"You're right. I should." Just then the phone rang.

I answered it. Michel put his wine glass down and continued paging through the album.

"Hello Robert."

"Irina, did I catch you at a good time?"

161

I looked over at Michel. "No. I'm sorry I can't talk right now. I'm with my son."

He gasped. "What?"

Michel looked up and smiled. I smiled back at him.

"Irina, what are you talking about? Your son?" He stuttered.

"I'll explain soon. I promise. Did you want something important?

His voice cracked. "To visit."

"I'm sorry, but I've got to go. Another time. Good-bye, Robert."

"But, but."

I ended the call and turned the ringer off. I hated to hang up on Robert, especially after seeing him with Monica, but I didn't want to lose any time with Michel.

Soon after, the timer went off in the kitchen. When all of the food was placed on the table, we sat down. Michel raised his glass to make a toast. "To new beginnings. And to you, my mother, to being reunited with you."

I smiled. "Thank you, Michel. And to you. I am incredibly happy."

We both took a sip of wine. We had expressed our happiness, our joy so many times in the past two days. I watched Michel as he ate and smiled at his entertaining stories about his life in France.

"Irina, do you realize you're staring at me?"

"Oh, I'm sorry. I'm thinking of the family resemblances. You have your grandfather's strong chin and forehead. Your father's build."

He smiled. "Speaking of which, do I have any living relatives in the United States?"

"You have second cousins living in Wisconsin. I have a cousin, Kay, in Sudbury Falls and she has two sons in their early thirties. Your grandfather's brother came over to

America shortly after he did. It feels strange talking about your father, your grandfather. My father."

"Yes, but isn't it wonderful?"

I nodded. It was wonderful. I reached my hand over to his and squeezed it.

Michel took another bite of the lasagna. "You're an excellent cook. This is outstanding." He put his fork down. "I put some thought into what we were discussing yesterday. About Alex. I could befriend him. He'll be at the club after work tomorrow and we're already acquaintances. He needs a new racquetball partner and I don't have a regular one. I could ask him if he'd like to be partners. I could try to get some information about him regarding Stephen. He might let something slip. You never know."

"Michel, I remember Tricia telling me that Alex was leaving on a business trip today. He wanted the funeral to be before that."

"That's not what I heard at the club. He needs a partner for this weekend."

I shrugged. So Alex lied to Tricia about being gone. "You'd have to be careful. He could be the murderer. He's on my list. I don't know if that's a great idea. "

Michel laughed. "Don't worry. I won't eat or drink anything he offers me."

I laughed, but it really wasn't funny.

"How else are you going to find out anything? Break into his home. Look for clues. Irina, somehow I just can't picture you doing that, a ballet dancer."

I raised my eyebrows.

He laughed again. He had a nice laugh.

Continuing to smile, I said, "Promise me you'll be careful."

He nodded. "I will."

"The cousin I spoke about earlier, Kay who lives in Wisconsin, she's a bit of a detective."

"Really?"

"Yes. She retired and moved back to Wisconsin and has solved a number of murder cases for the police."

Michel raised his eyebrows. "Interesting."

I shrugged. "Perhaps I should speak to her about Stephen. We haven't been in touch for a long time."

After dinner we had our dessert in the living room. I made carrot cake. When we had finished, I opened the gift wrapped package. Inside was the whimsical dragonfly cast iron teapot I had carefully picked out at Chelsea Market for Michel's "friend."

"What a surprise! Michel! How thoughtful!"

"It's to celebrate life's new beginnings."

"I love it, Michel." I gave him a hug and kiss. Tears filled my eyes.

He laughed and handed me his handkerchief. "I hope this isn't going to be a reoccurring thing with you. Crying every time we get together. I'll need to stock up on handkerchiefs."

I laughed and wiped my eyes. "I'm so happy." There was that word again.

We talked late into the evening about everything and anything: family, his new job, my life in the ballet, Robert, Stephen, Alex.

Close to midnight, Michel insisted on helping to clear everything from the table and we did the dishes. He offered to wash.

"Irina, where do you keep your trash?"

I pointed to a small closet in the corner of the kitchen. He picked up and opened the bag that held the items I had found in Stephen's trash.

"Not that bag. The one in the can next to it."

He pulled the water bottle from the bag. "This bottle. Bluebeat. I've seen it before."

"It's quite unusual. Where?"

"Stephen had one like it at the racquetball club. Come to think of it, so did Alex."

I didn't want to mention I had picked it from Stephen's trash. He had already mentioned that I would never break into someone's home.

Michel left to go back to his apartment just after one o'clock.

Chapter Sixteen

Friday, February 27

That morning, I put some notes I had been asked to look over for another grant, into my dark red leather tote and left for SAFE Shelter, an easy walk less than a mile away. Starting out, focusing on my breathing, I took in a deep breath, filling my lungs with air, then let it out. Mindfulness. It was easy being on the streets of the Upper West Side to focus my attention on the busy markets and shops I passed, taking my mind off of Stephen and Robert. I approached the shelter which was sandwiched between two tall concrete buildings. It was a nondescript place which would not easily attract attention from the abusers.

I had been volunteering at the shelter for several years, helping abused women fill out grant forms to get funding to aid in their starting over. The recipients could use the grant money for whatever was needed to help them get back on their feet: rent, transportation to a job, child care. I also helped them to apply for jobs online, coached them for interviews, and made sure they had appropriate clothing to wear for the interviews.

I unlocked the front door. After putting my things into the office and looking over the list of perspective grant applicants,

I headed for the shared living area where I would first socialize with the women and children. Afterwards, I would help with their grant applications. Most of the grant money was given by private individuals and foundations. I also had donated money and I knew other volunteers who did as well.

Entering the living area, a pretty girl around nine years old with perfect posture immediately came over to me. "Miss Irina. I didn't know you lived here."

I looked at the young girl and recognized her as a student I had a few years ago in my ballet studio. I smiled and said, "Hello Jennifer." Putting my hand on Jennifer's slender shoulder, I then looked for her mother and saw her sitting on a sofa which looked like it had seen better days.

Jennifer's mother looked down after we made eye contact. She had bruises on her arms. I thought about Tricia when I noticed bruises on her arms a couple of weeks ago. Then she came over to us and said, "I don't think Miss Irina lives here, Jenny."

After Jennifer left to help take care of the younger children, her mother said, "We arrived two days ago. I didn't want Jenny to witness my boyfriend's abuse any longer. And I had become afraid for her. I had passed this place many times, never thinking I would be here now, but here I am." She looked down. "We were told we can stay for a few weeks."

"I'm glad you came here. You made the right decision for Jenny and yourself." I gave the mother a hug, then looked her in the eye. "You're in a safe place."

"Thank you." She shifted weight from one foot to the other. "I don't know what we can do, how we are going to make it when we're out there again."

"I saw your name on the grant list. If you'd like, we could go to the office and get started filling out forms to try to help you get back on your feet." I smiled. I looked over at Jennifer. She was reading a book to some of the younger kids. "It seems Jennifer will be occupied for a while."

Jennifer's mother and I filled out the grant application and discussed what steps she could take to get her life back on track. Leaning in, she listened intently, her eyes focused when I told her the shelter's policy that all grant recipients were asked to "pay it forward", to perform acts of kindness for the other survivors, once they were back on their feet.

Clasping her hands under her chin in a prayer gesture she said, "What sort of acts of kindness?"

"Well, you could offer to help someone with child care or perhaps teach someone a new skill. Just *something* to help the others so they can manage a new life as well."

She nodded in agreement. "Thank you so much, Miss Irina. I better go and check on Jennifer."

I smiled as she got up to leave. These acts of kindness which the shelter insisted on, empowered the women to make them feel stronger and more confident, giving them a feeling of self-worth, by helping others.

I worked with two other women before leaving early afternoon.

* * * *

On the way to the ballet class, I thought about my dinner this evening with Charles. I looked forward to spending a relaxing time with him. Plus I wanted to learn what was going on with Stephen's investigation. By now, there should have been some progress made.

I arrived at the studio early. My plan was to have a frank talk with Jerome about Robert before the children came. For days I had been wondering, perhaps Robert was worth losing. My life was fine before he reentered the picture and he was starting to feel like a complication.

Sitting down on the piano bench next to Jerome, I said, "I've decided to end my relationship once and for all with Robert before it goes any further. I think it's the best thing to do."

He gave me an incredulous stare. Jerome was known to gossip, a lot. "I just spoke with Robert yesterday and —"

I took it that Robert and my relationship was the topic of their discussion. "It's not working out. I've decided to go to his apartment tomorrow to tell him. I don't want to do it over the phone or send him a 'Dear John' letter."

Jerome's posture stiffened. "You know I care about you. Are you sure this is what you want? I don't want to see you hurting like the last time you guys broke up."

"I'm sure about this. I've thought about it long and hard. It's for the best."

His posture relaxed.

"One positive thing that came out of this entire situation with Robert is that it has brought closure for me after all these years. I don't think I will ever shed another tear about his leaving me back in college, wondering why or what if."

Jerome smiled and hugged me, then played a few random notes on the piano.

I was happy Jerome accepted this. Now if only Robert would. I took in a deep breath, held it for a few seconds, then exhaled. I felt relief already, a weight lifted off my shoulders.

To change the subject I mentioned briefly about dinner with Michel at my home and then started talking about this afternoon's lesson.

The children started arriving after Jerome and I went through the music for the day's class. Ivy ran through the door holding a flower for me, her mother following. "Mother says I have tutu-love."

"Tutu love?"

She took off her coat and held her arms in fourth position, one arm raised high overhead and the other open to second position. "See, Miss Irina, I have a new tutu."

I smiled, looking between Ivy and her mother. I felt Ivy's exuberance, but the children were only allowed to wear their tights and leotards for class. "It's lovely, Ivy. You look as

169

radiant as the sun. But you need to save your tutu for special occasions, rehearsals and performances."

Ivy beamed as bright as her yellow tutu while her mother helped her out of it.

Turning in the direction of my sleeve being pulled, I gave my attention to Molly. "Miss Irina, I've been practicing my chassé all week."

"Fabulous, Molly. Perhaps you can lead us in that later."

Soon everyone arrived and Jerome started playing for our warm-up stretches.

As the recital music began and the children started in with the dance, I smiled as I saw the potential of the ballet hopefuls. I knew their dream of becoming a ballerina and saw their determination with each step. "Now, chassé across the floor. Molly will lead."

Molly smiled large.

* * * *

Charles picked me up in a taxi. I was surprised and pleased to learn we were going to his favorite French restaurant on West 47th Street. He definitely wasn't the Thai, Indian or Middle Eastern restaurant type, but I did enjoy the food at Le Antonin. I should take Michel there.

We were seated at an intimate table in the corner and given menus. This evening, after trying on several dresses, I chose a more daring than usual black-and-white print dress. I had bought the dress when shopping with Margarite. Looking around at the other patrons, I felt my choice was perfect for the venue.

I smiled at Charles when I noted the candlelight sparkle on the silver cutlery. I knew he was all about atmosphere: the lighting, the artwork on the walls, the spacing of tables, music. He loved the full experience. Charles ordered a sparkling wine. After the sommelier reverently showed him the bottle and uncorked it, he poured a small amount into his own glass and pre-tasted it. I glanced at the label. Langlois, Cremant De

Loire, Brut Rosé, N.V. France. Then Charles tasted the wine and nodded to show his approval of the approval. Not being an oenophile, I always thought this five-minute ritual, especially with the sommelier tasting the wine first, a bit pretentious and silly. When would they ever take the bottle back saying it was truly bad?

Charles was from old money. His family made their fortune in publishing, leaving behind an empire. Not wanting to follow in his father's and grandfather's footsteps, he entered the police academy right out of college to become one of "New York's Finest". But he was accustomed to the finer things in life, delighting in gourmet dining, designer clothes, a benefactor of the arts. Even though he loved all of those things, I didn't find him pretentious. He was the real deal. What you see is what you get.

Of course, I enjoyed dining out and loved art, music, and theatre, but over the years the finer things in life started to mean more. Things like reading a good book on a rainy day, the laughter of children in my studio, time spent in the company of good friends and *now* family, rather than going to elaborate parties on the New York scene.

After the sommelier left, Charles made a toast. "To a woman who has never lost her sense of wonder. To you, Irina, you make me see things that I've never noticed before."

I smiled and half-laughed. "Thank you, Charles. And to you." I couldn't think of any other way to respond.

I looked around the room. The purl of conversation was amiable with the occasional clinking of glasses and cutlery. When our appetizers arrived, Escargots a La Bourguignonne and Porcini Mushroom Tartlets, I smiled and said, "Well, isn't this lovely. Much better than a quick bite to eat before the movie."

"The movie doesn't start until ten o'clock. We have plenty of time."

171

I was surprised when Charles cooled the warm ambiance after such a thoughtful toast and said, "So Irina, please tell me you're not getting back with Robert."

I could feel my heart starting to pound. "It's not going to happen with him."

Charles reached for my hand. "I'm relieved. I still say he wasn't up to your caliber."

I wanted to change the subject, but Charles added, "Do you think he might be in Manhattan doing something shifty? He seemed that type to me."

"Shifty?" I laughed, happy to feel relaxed again. "You're such a cop. Are you seeing anyone special?"

A silly grin appeared on his face. "I'm with a special lady right now."

I could feel myself blushing even though we were only good friends. "Oh Charles, you're so sweet." I took a bite of the escargot. It was bursting with flavor, garlic and butter. I loved the flavor. It was easy to do mindfulness concentrating on the garlic and butter.

He leaned in. "Your complexion matches the color of the wine."

I laughed again. "Sweet talker." I took a sip. Next I took a turn shattering the relaxed atmosphere. "Is there any progress with the investigation?"

"Please Irina, I don't want to ruin this evening."

Our entrées arrived. I had ordered Sautéed Sea Scallops in White Wine. Charles, Grilled Breast of Duck. The presentation was beautiful.

While eating, I brought up the subject of Stephen again. "I've been thinking about the flowers in Stephen's —." I stopped before saying 'stomach contents.' "It wouldn't have been suicide. I doubt he would have eaten flowers if he had decided to do away with himself with the antifreeze."

Charles took another bite of his "crisp-to-perfection" duck, keeping his eyes down. "We are quickly approaching closure of the case."

"Really?" I said a bit too loudly. People looked in our direction. "You found the murderer then?" I then said softly.

Charles took another bite. When he had finished swallowing, he said, "No. That's not what I'm saying."

My eyebrows drew together. "What exactly are you saying, if you're not considering this murder? You know his wife is going to have him cremated and that will be the end of it."

He reached for his wine glass. "Even if he were cremated at this point, it wouldn't matter. We were given a document. Stephen belonged to The River Styk Society."

"The River Styk Society? What's that?"

"It's a branch of the Hemlock Society, the Compassion and Choices Organization, the right-to-die society. With his being deadly sick these past months—"

I put my fork down. "Only when he was home. And he *wasn't* dying."

"His case is looking like a suicide. Irina, let's not spoil this evening."

"Stephen wasn't suicidal. I told you he was excited about this job promotion. He wasn't the type to belong to any River Styk Society. That's absurd. Alice, his sister-in-law probably added him to the ledger. Did she provide the document?" My eyes started to brim with tears. "And where was his suicide note? There wasn't one!"

Charles cut another piece of his duck. He said quietly, "Don't work yourself up or accuse anyone. I didn't say his sister-in-law provided us with the document."

"And you're not denying it." I reached into my purse, took out Michel's soft, white handkerchief, and dabbed my eyes. "One *last* thing. Stephen was in stiff competition with an office-mate Alex Rankin for the new position in their ad

173

agency. It was a huge salary increase. I've been talking to Stephen's widow. Seems like Alex may have been the type to eliminate his competition."

Charles put down his fork and took a drink of his wine. "I hope you'll enjoy the movie tonight. I'm looking forward to it."

I could feel my face redden. Well, that was it. Charles wasn't going to say anything else about Stephen. It didn't seem like the police were going to help any further in the investigation. I hoped Michel would be able to come up with something on Alex this evening at the racquetball club.

We ended the meal sharing a piece of Gateau au Chocolat, French chocolate cake and left for the movie.

Chapter Seventeen

Saturday, February 28

I slept in late, having not gotten home until almost two o'clock. Charles wanted to stop off for a drink after the movie. That was where I told him about Michel being my son. Across the bedroom I saw the light on the answering machine flashing. I hadn't noticed it last night.

It was Robert. "Irina, I was thinking about you this evening. Wondering what you were doing this weekend, what your plans were? Please give me a call. I hope you'll be free to get together Saturday evening or Sunday." His voice sounded hopeful. Breaking off our relationship might be harder to do than I thought. As soon as I showered and dressed I would go to Robert's apartment and end our relationship, making it as quickly and painlessly as possible.

The mile plus walk along the Riverside Park Greenway was always beautiful with gorgeous views of the river. This morning I barely noticed my surroundings walking to Robert's apartment, continually rehearsing in my mind exactly what I was going to say. I would say what I had to and make it fast. When I reached Robert's apartment building, a man was just leaving and held the heavy glass door open for me. I entered the plush lobby. Three people sat behind the desk. The doorman must have recognized me from my previous visit, came up, and greeted me as I walked toward the elevator.

I knocked twice on Robert's door. Close to a minute later, he opened the door looking a bit disheveled with his shirt unbuttoned and hair messed up. I hoped he wasn't feeling ill this morning, to make this even harder for me.

Frowning he asked, "Irina, what are you doing here?" He wiped his mouth with the back of his hand.

"I heard your message this morning. There's something I need to discuss with you. Can I come into your apartment?"

Robert inched further into the hallway closing the door behind him. "What did you want to see me about?"

"Please, I'd really rather talk to you inside. It's rather personal and very important."

He grimaced. "This isn't a good time for me. I caught a bug and might be contagious."

He was sick. I didn't have the heart to terminate our relationship if he was feeling ill. "Oh, I'm sorry to hear that. Perhaps you'll be feeling better tomorrow. We can talk then."

He managed a smile. "Yes. That would be a good idea. I'll call you tomorrow. Goodbye."

I heard a sound coming from behind the door. I leaned in towards Robert, but before I even looked around him to see who was starting to open the door, I could smell Monica's cheap scent on him. Okay, maybe the perfume wasn't cheap, but she was.

"Robert?" Monica opened the door, saw me, and smiled. A confident, cocky smile.

"Hello Irina. Robert didn't tell me you were joining us, again." She then put her hand on Robert's shoulder. "Robert could you do a girl a favor and zip up the back of my dress?"

I looked from Monica's mocking eyes fixed on me, to Robert's. "A bug? Yes, I can see that." Then I looked back to Monica. She continued to look pleased with herself, her bright red, botoxed lips smiling in overkill. After Robert zipped her

176

dress she went back into the apartment leaving the door open wide and flung herself on a leather chair near the entryway, her body language as uninhibited as the rest of her. Her legs crossed, she swung her stiletto shoe with its bondage strap, barely missing a glass-topped table. Her breasts protruded, showing much cleavage from yet another low-cut, short dress that was decades too young for her.

Suddenly everything became crystal clear.

Robert came back out into the hall and shut the door to his apartment again. I watched his Adam's apple bob up and down as he said, "Irina, I can explain."

How could anyone explain that? I looked at Robert, then turned and started for the elevator. He grabbed on to my hand. I pulled my hand away from his.

He put his hands behind his back. "Please, Irina. I did ask you out for every night this week." He kept firm eye contact. "You were never available." He continued in a hushed voice, then turned towards his apartment and pointed towards the door, "She means nothing. Nothing." His lip curled.

They had just had sex and she meant nothing to him. I shook my head. What a disgusting person he was. I stared at the elevator floor indicators.

"You're the one who is warm and inviting. You draw me in. Not her."

I glanced at him. When he turned to the side looking towards his apartment, I saw that red lipstick stained his jaw and side of his neck.

I pressed the down button of the elevator again, then reached in my pocket. Taking out a tissue, I was about to hand it to him and tell him to wipe his face, but why bother. He was such an arrogant bastard. The doors opened. I turned abruptly and entered the elevator.

It was over.

* * * *

I knocked on Margarite's door when I got back to the apartment.

"Why didn't I see this coming? It's over. I need to get control of myself."

Margarite squinted her eyes. "A mindfulness concept?"

"No. I can't believe what a snake Robert is!"

Still looking puzzled, she said, "You'd better come in."

I followed her into the kitchen.

"Irina, I've never seen your shoulders slump before. You've always had perfect posture. What's wrong?" Offering me a glass of wine, she went into a cupboard, took two glasses out and put them on the table.

I straightened out my posture. I said, "Are those both for me? One glass wouldn't be enough." Then I laughed and declined the wine. "It's a bit early." I felt a release when I laughed.

We sat down at her kitchen table. I told her about Robert, how shallow and insincere he was and Charles' assessment of him and how I had planned to break up with Robert. "You'd think I would have known better. Why didn't I see this earlier? There were signs."

Margarite offered a deep sigh and reached across the table and squeezed my hand. "Are you sure you don't want that wine?" She laughed then shook her head. "Irina, you only see the good in people. You're better off without him. Charles was right, Robert isn't up to your caliber."

"Of course I'm better off without him. That's why I went over to his apartment." My eyes watered a little. "He's a closed book. I'm incredibly sorry for Todd, Monica's partner. And Monica. She's like Odile from Swan Lake." Even though I felt emotionally drained, like in a void, I still felt my tension lifting.

Margarite laughed. "Monica and Robert deserve each other. You'll get over it."

I nodded and leaned back, with an arm hooked over the chair. "I know I will."

Margarite offered to make coffee when I declined the wine again.

While we waited for the coffee, I started telling Margarite about Michel's attempt to befriend Alex. The doorbell interrupted our conversation.

I poured the coffee while Margarite answered her door. I could hear Tricia's voice and went into the living room over to them.

"Good, you're both here. I wanted to let you know Stephen's funeral will be on Monday at eleven o'clock. His body has been released to the funeral home. The case is closed. They're calling his death a suicide."

Tricia looked relieved. How could she?

With my jaw clenching, I struggled to find the right words, then asked, "Do you honestly believe that, that Stephen committed suicide?"

She shrugged irritably. "Since the funeral is such short notice, the luncheon will be at our home afterwards. We are having it catered by Parsley and Sage. They have fabulous food."

This was your husband, Tricia. How could you even accept this ruling? You're told Stephen committed suicide and all you talk about is the funeral luncheon. "I don't believe Stephen committed suicide for one minute."

Tricia looked over at Margarite, then down at her feet, sliding a foot back and forth. "His death has been called a suicide, Irina. We're having the funeral on Monday. Stephen's sister is anxious to go back home."

"Just because your sister said Stephen was a member of the Styks Society—"

Tricia's face tightened. "What business is it of yours if she told the police that? Come if you want on Monday. I really don't care." She turned on her heels and headed towards her apartment.

"What do you make of that?" I asked Margarite after she closed the door.

"Tricia either wants this business to be over with or else she's the killer. And she's definitely fed up with you."

"So Alice was the person who gave the police the document. I wasn't sure about that until now. Charles wouldn't tell me."

"That was a clever way to find out."

We went back into the kitchen and I sank into the chair. "This is terrible. I can't believe there won't be any justice for Stephen. We both know he didn't commit suicide. How can Tricia even live with herself?"

After Margarite finished her coffee, I couldn't drink anymore, I went back to my apartment and called Charles. He didn't pick up. I left a message letting him know that Stephen's funeral was on Monday and that I thought he should be there.

* * * *

Early evening, Michel gave me a call. "I played racquetball with Alex yesterday. It happened he was looking for a partner."

"Did you find out anything?"

"Alex had the same Bluebeat water bottle that Stephen had. I asked him about the brand. He said it's a company in Chicago. He's from Chicago. My guess is Stephen's bottle was given to him by Alex."

I raised my eyebrows. "Interesting, Michel. Did you get a chance to look in his locker?"

"I glanced in it when we were changing clothes. I didn't see anything incriminating. He invited me over this evening to look at his extensive jazz record collection. Perhaps I'll notice something there.

You're our last hope. "Be careful. And don't drink anything he gives you."

"Yes, Mother. I remember you telling me that previously."

We both hesitated. I smiled. I told Michel about the antifreeze being the murder weapon.

"I should get ready to leave. I'll check around for antifreeze, although if I see any, you do realize that's a common substance," he said.

After we hung up I thought about Michel calling me "Mother" even if it wasn't how he meant it. The word sounded wonderful and gave me such a thrill. I felt joyful. I did a twirl where I was standing.

My mind went back to yesterday when I had googled antifreeze and learned that it smelled like pancake or maple syrup and had a sweet taste. I put on kitchen gloves and picked out the Bluebeat bottle from the bag that contained Tricia's garbage contents. I opened the bottle and smelled the substance. There was a small amount of liquid left in it. It smelled sweet. But how could that be distinguished from Gatorade. Gatorade and antifreeze were the same color.

How do I convince Charles to have the contents of this bottle analyzed now that the death had been declared a suicide? Was it still possible that he would? I was definitely going to ask.

I went across the hall to Tricia's and knocked on her door. I stared at the brass peephole and saw a shadow, someone inside looking through it. I had taken a chance, when I was on the other side of Tricia's door peeping out at Celeste that day, when Margarite and I discovered Stephen's nootropics. She might have noticed someone on the other side of the door.

Tricia answered, not looking all that pleased to see me. I told her I was sorry about coming on too strong previously, that I had had a bad day.

She managed to produce a half-smile. "Come in, Irina. I'm working on a eulogy. Remember, the funeral luncheon is here directly after the service. I don't imagine there will be many people here with the short notice."

"Could I bring something, perhaps a dessert?"

"Thank you, but I've already ordered everything."

"Tricia, the other day when I was taking my garbage downstairs, I noticed a unique water bottle. I believe it said Bluebeat on the bottle. Was that Stephen's?"

Her eyes widened. "Alice told me she saw you digging around in our garbage containers. I didn't believe her." As soon as she said that she immediately covered her mouth with her hand. "I'm sorry, Irina. It seems like all kinds of things are coming out of my mouth lately also."

"Actually I *was* digging in the garbage. I had lost a drug prescription and thought perhaps it had fallen into the garbage when I was cooking."

"Stephen brought the bottle home from racquetball the evening before he died. We have so many water bottles. I threw it out when we were cleaning the apartment."

Probably before the ambulance came when their kitchen was spotless.

Her brows pulled together. "I didn't know why he didn't take one from home. We certainly didn't need another to add to our collection."

Alice came into the room with her usual dismal expression on her face. "Did you take the bottle?"

Alice had been listening. "Hello Alice." I turned back to Tricia. "Margarite and I will both be at the funeral on Monday and the luncheon afterwards. Please let me know if there is anything I can do to help."

I quickly left without answering Alice's question. Interesting, that she would care about the bottle.

182

Chapter Eighteen

Sunday, March 1

I was sitting in the kitchen, slowly eating a bowl of granola mixed with fruit, trying to concentrate on the texture of the cereal when I crunched down. The sweetness of the organic strawberries and blueberries enveloped my mouth.

Rrrring Rrrring Rrrring.

As much as I tried, I was never going to fully get into this mindfulness. My mind was always wandering. I went and answered the phone. "Hello."

"Irina, Alex has a car. A Lexus. We went for a ride to New Jersey to a jazz club he frequents." It was Michel, his voice sounded excited.

"Great! That answers our question then, he would have antifreeze."

He continued, sounding even more excited now. "His car is always serviced, so he wouldn't specifically have a need, but I saw a partially used jug of it under the sink when I searched his bathroom."

My eyes opened wide. I sat down again at the kitchen table. This was a bigger jolt than I got from my last two cups of coffee. "Fantastic! You found the means! Great work. And we have a motive and the opportunity."

"Yes! So what's the next step?"

"Charles. Charles is the next step."

"I thought he said the case was closed?" Michel said in a questioning voice.

I smiled large. "Not for long."

* * * *

Since it was Sunday, I called Charles to see if he was home. Receiving an affirmative answer, I took the subway and walked a few blocks to his apartment in SoHo. A chic neighborhood of trendy upscale shops, art galleries, and great restaurants greeted me with the energy of a middle-of-the week day. I had a spring in my step as I approached Charles' brownstone.

Charles welcomed me into his home with a big smile and a warm hug. He was dressed neatly, but casually wearing an open collar shirt, a forest green sweater, and khakis. I kissed him on his well-shaven cheek. I could faintly smell his cologne. Soft jazz music was playing in the background. I looked around. Endless books lined two of the walls of his living room. Works of art lined another.

"To what do I owe this pleasure?" He returned my kiss.

I smiled back, warmth radiating through my body, and took the water bottle out of a paper bag, still wearing my winter gloves. "This was a unique water bottle given to Stephen by Alex Rankin at the racquetball club. I believe it contains the antifreeze that killed him. Alex has a car that is serviced, but also had antifreeze in his home."

Charles feigned a sad look. "Oh, Irina. And here I thought you were coming to see me. What makes you think that it's antifreeze in the bottle?"

"Michel. He saw antifreeze in Alex's apartment."

He reached for the bottle.

I put the bottle back in the bag. "I think it should be checked for fingerprints and see if this bottle does indeed hold the murder weapon. There's still a small amount of liquid in it."

He laughed. "Irina, you do, do you? You're relentless. You realize that, don't you? As much as I should be annoyed, I love that about you. You never give up. Not ever!" He gave me another hug, a warm bear hug.

"Not when my friend has been *murdered*. And the water bottle, it was the timing. Stephen was given this bottle by Alex the day before he died."

Charles took the bag. "Okay, I'll take this in later today. Consider it done. But know, this is the last time. If nothing turns up, you must finally conclude that this case remains closed."

"Agreed." Mentally I had my fingers crossed. "Stephen's funeral is tomorrow. Are you planning on going? The murderer may be there."

"We'll see."

"I think you should."

Charles smiled, took my coat, and mumbled, "relentless" when hanging it up.

I smiled. "What smells so good?"

"When you called and said you were coming over, I threw together a Quiche Lorraine. It still has another forty minutes to bake. I hope you'll stay for brunch."

"I'd love to. Thank you."

"Great. Let's go into kitchen and have a cup of coffee. I planned on making a spinach and strawberry salad."

"I'll help you with that."

Charles' sleek kitchen with bleached floors had all clean lines, stainless steel appliances and bar stools under the island. The bright breakfast room opened out onto a garden. Golden light was streaming through the French doors.

"I love this room." I went over to the French doors and looked out. "And how fabulous it must be in the summer having coffee in the mornings on your deck with this beautiful view."

"Perhaps you'll find out for yourself this coming summer."

I shrugged, not knowing how to respond, or if I even should respond.

Working side by side in the kitchen felt comfortable with Charles. I watched him smiling as he readied the salad. He was one of my oldest and dearest friends. We had much in common and ever since I'd known Charles, he had always watched out for me. I think we belonged to the mutual admiration society.

With the table already set for two, we sat down to a glorious brunch complete with Prosecco. Charles raised his glass and said, "To us."

Charles had always been careful with his speech, choosing his words carefully. I smiled in agreement. "To us."

"And to a woman who loves life. May it always be filled with love."

I raised my eyebrows. I never knew how to respond to Charles' toasts.

He took a sip of the Prosecco and then put down his glass. "I'm thinking about retiring, Irina, and feeling optimistic about starting my next chapter. I've been thinking also about you as well. I hope you'll be part of it. I'd like you to be part of it."

I felt a blush come to my cheeks. Feeling needed, feeling wanted. I liked that. "Charles, I've always been a part of your life and will remain so. You know that."

He nodded. "And I'm grateful that you are. Life is wonderful with you in it and can get even better. We have the best years of our lives ahead of us." His eyes softened, fixating on mine.

Over the years I hadn't much contemplated about Charles in terms of a romance. We had a connection both intellectually and I'd have to admit physically. There was always a kind of spark between us, that was never acted on. Was it time to let it ignite? I was comfortable with Charles, that wasn't a question, and we loved many of the same things. He was a great friend and we did fun things together. But a partner? Was I too idealistic, always looking for something in life that wasn't going to be there? It definitely wasn't with Robert.

He smiled. "This is starting to sound like a Hallmark card, Irina."

I laughed. "It is, isn't it?"

He reached for my hand. "I think we're good together."

I smiled again and reached my hand to his across the table. He squeezed it gently. "I agree. I think we are also." I did mean that.

Later when we were eating, I mentioned about the theft of Margarite's vase. I left out the part about finding it in the garbage when I was searching for clues.

"I know about the theft."

I raised my eyebrows. "Really, a New York Police Lieutenant, with all that is going on in the city, and you know about her vase being stolen?" If he knew that, he probably also knew it was found broken in the garbage by me.

"Irina, I have been keeping a watch out for you and your safety for years. When anything happens in your immediate area, the police have been advised to contact me. We are watching the neighborhood. It seems most of the items reported stolen have been smaller items. Antiques, jewelry, a silver powder box, although there are exceptions. A coin collection has gone missing and art. The thefts always take place when the occupants are away."

"That would lead me to think that the criminal knows the people he's stealing from. He knows when they will be home and when they'll be away."

"Exactly. He or she seems to have a handle on that information. That's all I can tell you for now."

We finished our meal over great conversation and before I left, Charles kissed me goodbye, this time not on my cheek, but on my lips. A soft, warm kiss.

"Thank you again for the lovely brunch."

He smiled. "It was my pleasure. Please stop by anytime."

As I was walking down the hall to the entrance he called out, "I mean that, Irina. Anytime. Anytime at all."

I smiled and opened the door. "See you tomorrow. Don't forget about the water bottle."

Charles smiled and gently shook his head. "How could I?"

On the way to the subway station, I thought about how much more pleasant this visit was than when I had stopped by at Robert's.

* * * *

In the train on the way home, my thoughts went to what life might be like with Charles. My daydreaming was disturbed by the sound of my cell phone ringing.

"Irina, something is going on in Tricia and Alice's apartment. I heard arguing, even screaming."

A man with a trim white beard wearing a dark herringbone ivy cap was standing right next to me. He was reading the newspaper with one hand hanging onto the pole in front of him. I said quietly, "Margarite, could you hear what they were saying?"

"Something about the water bottle. You should have heard the intensity of the voices. I went back into my apartment. Irina, their door just slammed."

"Did you hear my name mentioned?"

"No, but then I couldn't hear every word."

"Look out the peephole," I said a bit too loudly. The man reading never took his eyes off the paper.

"Too late. Hang on."

"Be careful."A woman sitting with a young child looked across at me. "Margarite?" She wasn't there. The cell phone was cutting in and out. The connection was terrible.

188

"Margarite?"

After about a half minute, Margarite came back on. She sounded out of breath. "Irina, it was Alex Rankin. He just stormed out the front door."

"Alex was there also? Who did the screaming? Are you back in your apartment?"

"Yes. It was mostly Alex and Alice."

Margarite sounded out of breath.

Alex and Alice? "Stay in your apartment," I said.

"I wonder what that was about?"

"The bottle," I said. "It was about the water bottle. Alex knows the bottle could be some damning evidence. I wonder if Alice saw me pick it out of the garbage?"

Chapter Nineteen

Monday, March 2

Stephen's funeral was held in the Novak Funeral Chapel on West 72nd Street. Margarite had taken off of work and I postponed ballet class that afternoon until Wednesday. I wasn't sure how long the luncheon would last and didn't think I would be in a mood to dance anyway.

Tricia and Stephen's sister greeted Margarite, Michel, and me when we arrived. It wasn't a large affair. A few people were standing around visiting. I questioned the light attendance, since I was sure Stephen had many friends. Tricia and Alice might have wanted to keep his funeral a lower profile and didn't notify them of the new date. Perhaps they were embarrassed the date had been changed often and wouldn't want to explain about the body not being released for so long.

Facing the podium, there were several rows of chairs that would now be empty. Next to the podium, the urn that contained Stephen's ashes sat on a vintage mahogany table in the heavily draped room. A spray of lush flowers and foliage surrounded the urn.

While I was visiting with Margarite and a few neighbors, Charles showed up in plain clothes. I was relieved to see him walk through the door. I knew he'd keep his eyes open. He noticed me and smiled, then went over and talked with Trisha a few minutes. When he came over to us, I introduced him to Michel. They visited and got on well. I was happy about that. I hoped it wasn't a mistake that Michel was with us. He assured me he would leave as soon as Alex showed up.

Alex arrived with several people wearing business suits who I imagined he worked with and who had worked with Stephen. When Michel noticed Alex come into the funeral home, he went straight over to talk with him. Alex did a double-take when Michel approached him while he waited to speak with Tricia. I supposed Michel would explain his presence at the funeral as knowing Stephen from the racquetball club. I pointed out Alex to Charles. After a while Alex appeared relaxed talking with Michel. It looked like he had taken Michel's attendance in stride. Alice also joined their group.

Soon the service started. Everyone took their seats. Margarite and I sat close to the back, wanting to observe everyone. Charles sat in the row in front of us. Naturally, Tricia and Stephen's sister sat in the first row. Alice and Alex behind them. I shook my head. What an appropriate coupling, Alice and Alex. Michel sat behind Alex.

A minister presided and led a few prayers while standing beside the urn that held Stephen's ashes. I squinted my eyes and stared at the flowers surrounding the urn. I hadn't looked closely at them before.

After the minister finished, I said quietly to Margarite, "Are those blue delphiniums among the mix of the spray by the urn? Tricia and Alice wouldn't have included those in the spray, would they?"

"Could be one final last blow," she responded.

I felt the blood vessel in my temple starting to pulsate. Oh, Stephen. I was so sorry I couldn't bring you justice.

Fighting back tears, Tricia stood behind the podium next and said a few words, speaking about losing a husband far too early in life and how much she loved Stephen. I didn't know how everyone else felt, but she didn't sound convincing to me. Soon her tears became sobs and she lost total control, tears streaming down her cheeks.

"Do you suppose this is some kind of spectacle on Tricia's part to confirm her innocence?" Margarite whispered.

I shrugged and shook my head slowly.

Stephen's sister came up and put her arms around Tricia, who clung to her for a couple of minutes before Tricia returned to her seat.

Next, Stephen's sister spoke longer, being more in control and with heart. When she talked about what a wonderful older brother Stephen was, how she had always looked up to him, and shared a few amusing stories, I nodded and teared up. It was incredibly sad. Stephen was gone and it looked like his murder would never be solved.

The final blessings were given to sobs coming from Tricia and Stephen's sister. I hated to think this and knew it unkind, but one seemed real and the other put-on. Again, this all made me quite sad, because Stephen truly was a wonderful person. A tear rolled down my cheek. I glanced at Alice when she turned around to leave. She was dry-eyed. I looked down as she passed by.

After the funeral, I invited Charles, Michel, and Margarite to stop off at my apartment for a glass of wine before going on to Tricia's. It was an opportunity for everyone to collect their thoughts on the situation. Charles politely listened, but didn't add much to the conversation.

"Michel, did you get any kind of feeling from Alex? Was he surprised to see you?"

"He seemed to accept my being there, having known Stephen from the Club, but mentioned he didn't realize Stephen and I were friends. Throughout the eulogies, he picked at his cuticles when he wasn't looking at his watch. Talk about distracting."

Margarite stood up. "Well, should we get this show on the road."

Her comment took me by surprise, sounding a bit hard.

With the coast clear in the hallway, Michel left to go across the hall first, so he wouldn't arrive with us. Charles and I finished our wine and the three of us followed a few minutes later.

It looked like we were the late comers. Most everyone I remembered who had attended the service was already in the apartment. Small tables were spread out in the living and dining rooms. We found a table close to the kitchen. Michel was already seated, along with Alex and a few others Alex came to the funeral with.

Parsley and Sage catered the luncheon, a fabulous catering establishment on the Upper West Side. Beautiful fruit and vegetable platters were displayed on the dining table. I recognized a Moroccan spiced chicken platter served with pita bread, I previously had at an event. Glazed pork tenderloin medallions were served on cream biscuits and a plate of sesame-crusted salmon completed the main dishes. Off to one side of the table was an array of luscious desserts.

Celeste from upstairs, and a couple of the neighbors from the next brownstone joined us at our table. Charles talked with Celeste quite a bit while I kept my eye on Alex. Tricia and Alice sat with Stephen's sister and two of Tricia's friends from the Met. I had been to a party at Tricia's last year and recognized them. I couldn't understand why Charles seemed more interested in talking to Celeste than watching the others, my suspects. I listened for a moment. Their conversation concerned a play that was starting next month off Broadway. Margarite soon joined in on the conversation. Blocking out their conversation, I kept alert as to what was going on with everyone in the room, something I felt Charles should have been doing. Nothing was out of the ordinary, until there was a knock on the door about a half hour after we sat down.

When Alice opened the door, I was surprised to see Robert walk through.

Charles looked at me. "I thought Robert was over."

I grated my teeth and smiled, "He is."

"Then what's he doing here?"

"I have no idea," I said through my teeth.

Robert looked across the room over to me and then went over to Tricia, I assumed to give his condolences. When they were finished talking he looked in my direction. Not wanting him to come over to our table and make a scene, because I didn't know how Charles would respond, I got up and went over to him. I noticed Charles stood up as well, but remained at the table.

Robert smiled at me. "Hello, Irina. Before you say anything, I want to apologize again about the other day. Please believe me when I say it meant nothing. You mean *everything* to me. No great love ever came without great struggle."

I felt like rolling my eyes, but restrained myself. I started walking towards the door to get out of earshot of the others in the room. Not being able to ignore his ridiculous, trite comment, I said quietly crossing my arms, "What is that some famous quote?"

Robert sighed heavily. "No. It's how I feel. I hope you can forgive me. I want to be in your life."

It was a quote. I had heard it before. "Robert I came over to your apartment *that* morning to tell you we are over."

His mouth fell open.

I narrowed my eyes. "Do you even realize how insulting you are to come here today? Love requires respect. Please, Robert, please just leave."

When I turned around to return to my seat, Charles was a short distance behind me, his eyebrows drawn together.

When I reached him, he said, "I thought you might need a little help."

I looked up at Charles and smiled. "Thank you. I'm fine."

Charles looked past me at Robert, his eyes cold, his mouth pressed tightly.

When we sat back down, Charles took my hand under the table, squeezed it, and smiled. I smiled, then glanced back toward Robert who was retreating out the door.

The conversation soon went back to other plays Celeste, Margarite, and Charles had enjoyed. While taking a sip of water, I noticed Alex go into the kitchen. Tricia and Alice were talking to Stephen's sister on the other side of the room.

I put my glass down and walked over to the kitchen, and stood near the doorway. Alex was opening the cupboard doors systematically. Was he looking for the Bluebeat water bottle? Had Tricia or Alice not mentioned that I had seen the bottle in the garbage? Perhaps they were too worried during his fit of anger the other day, when Margarite had overheard him, to have mentioned that. Margarite said he was enraged at the time.

Alex glanced in my direction with a pinched expression when I entered the room.

"Can I help you find something?" I asked.

"You're the neighbor I saw in the hallway when I was picking up Stephen."

"Yes, that was me."

Alex looked back toward the cupboards. "I'm looking for a glass."

He thought the glasses would be in a lower cupboard? "There are several on the buffet in the other room." I opened the door to the last cupboard he had just looked in. "Here are more."

Alex looked me up and down, then chuckled nervously. "So they are." He took a glass and turned on the sink. "Some of the food served is quite spicy."

I watched him while he drank a full glass of water.

"It's incredibly sad, Stephen's death. We were close, almost like brothers."

I forced a smile. What a loser.

Tricia entered the room. Alex turned to her saying, "Tricia, I hope you'll be okay. Remember, you can call on me if you need anything." He put his hand on her shoulder, rubbing it.

"Thank you. I will." She looked over at me and blushed. Then gave a half-smile and shrugged her shoulder. She moved away from Alex, his arm dropping.

Alice appeared and went over to Alex. He held his hand out to her.

I raised my eyebrows. What was the deal with Tricia and Alex? Alex was way too familiar for my liking. Tricia had mentioned she and Stephen were friends with Alex but how good of friends were they? Was there more to them than I knew about? Or Stephen had known about? She appeared to be embarrassed that Alex squeezed her shoulder. Was it because I was in the room or because she didn't like his advances? Who was Alex here for, Tricia or Alice? Had I been wrong about Alice, and perhaps Tricia was more the power behind Stephen's death?

Leaving the kitchen bewildered, I heard Alex mention the water bottle. Lurking outside the door, I heard Alice mention my name. Instantly a shiver of fear ran through me.

I went back to my table, half-listening to the conversation taking place while keeping my eyes on the kitchen. A few minutes later, Alex, Tricia, and Alice returned to their respective tables. A slightly smug smile surfaced on Alex's mouth when he looked over at my table. His look was brief, but returned several times throughout the luncheon. With each glance, my heart raced faster until I could hear its beat in my ears.

Did Alex knew I was sitting next to a police officer? A police officer I had given the water bottle to. I put my hand on Charles' arm. Charles looked over at me, smiled, then continued talking to Celeste. What was with that?

People started leaving. When Charles, Margarite, and I got up to leave, I noticed everyone at Alex's table had already vacated.

Chapter Twenty

Tuesday, March 3

When I opened my door to take out the garbage, Alex Rankin was standing in the hallway in front of me with an intent expression. "Alice told me yesterday you have something of mine."

I could think of only one thing that he wanted. "I have no idea what you are talking about. I have nothing of yours." I tried to get past him. He didn't move. "I'm sorry, but I'm short on time. Please excuse me, I'm heading out for an appointment after I take this garbage down."

He pushed me backwards into my apartment. "I think *that* will have to wait. You're not going anywhere until you give *it* to me."

Shocked by his unflickering stare, a chill passed through me in spite of my heavy winter coat. The bag of garbage fell out of my arms, it's contents spilling out in my foyer, as I recoiled in intense and helpless fear.

"What do you think you're doing, Alex Rankin?"

Alex loomed above me, blocking any way past him. "You have the water bottle I lent Stephen. I want it back."

I decided I could try to play it nonchalantly. "Water bottle? Is that what you're getting so worked up about? A *water bottle?"* Oh no, he knew I had the murder weapon. Was I about to become his next victim?

I then tried to force my way back to the door and screamed, "Help! Help!" the door still being open.

He pulled me back and slammed the door, standing in front of it. "Shut up! I know you have it."

I kicked him in the shin as hard as I could and backed away into the living room. My cell phone was in my purse that was hanging on my shoulder, but that would have taken time to get out to make a call. "I don't have whatever water bottle it is that you are talking about." Then I screamed, "Get out of my home!" as loud as I could. I didn't know who would hear me. Margarite was at school. If Tricia and Alice were at home, would they even respond if they were conspiring with this psychotic guy?

He moved towards me with eyes that burned with intensity, forcing me to retreat farther into the house.

I grabbed the phone sitting on the buffet, ran behind the dining room table, trying to punch in 9-1-1 as fast as I could.

It wasn't fast enough. Alex closed the gap and ripped the phone cord out of the wall. The vase with Michel's flowers fell over, shattering on the floor, sending a cascade of water flowing across the room. I screamed again.

Trying to buy time, I said, "Was the antifreeze in the water bottle? The antifreeze that killed Stephen? Is that why you want the bottle?"

His eyes widened briefly, then narrowed again. Now he knew that I knew. He pushed the table hard in my direction, pinning me against the wall and preventing me from moving.

"Do Tricia and Alice know you poisoned Stephen?" I said with the last of my breath, as the table squeezed harder.

"Aren't you the clever one? Alice warned me about you. I needed Stephen out of the picture. She was taking too long. Too bad you won't be able to tell anyone. Now where is it?"

He was confessing. That only meant one thing for me. Just as he said, I wouldn't be around to tell. At this point, I had nothing to lose. But what could I do?

The table's pressure released as Alex turned and made his way around it, toward me. He pulled me out from behind the table and covered my mouth with his hand when I tried to scream again. I elbowed him in his side, remembering from a self-defense class that the elbow was the strongest offensive weapon on my body. Alex doubled up in pain, and I took the opportunity to run back into the living room towards the door and open it. But he wasn't incapacitated for long. Before I knew it, he again sped toward me in an instant, slamming the door with his foot, then locking it. Now I was trapped. Turning slowly toward me, he grabbed my throat with his sweaty hands, breathing hard. We went backward, deeper into the house again. I felt a brief pressure on my shoulder, followed by a loud, startling crash. My feet crunched as I continued backward over the shards of my broken stained glass floor lamp.

"Give it to me!"

By some miracle, the next thing that happened was the front door slamming open with the sound of splintering wood. Alex's head whipped behind him to address this unexpected noise. Startled myself, but not wanting to waste this new opportunity, I executed my best *grande battlement*, kicking Alex in the groin and doubling him up on the floor. I gave it to him, all right.

Charles had kicked the door in and now had the prone Alex pinned to the ground. Then he cuffed him, and it was over. I collapsed onto a chair, breathing a sigh of relief.

Turning to me he said, "Irina, are you okay? Your neck."

I coughed, fingering my tender throat. "I'm fine. Thank goodness you came when you did."

Charles called for backup, then read Alex his rights.

"Alex Rankin, you're under arrest for the murder of Stephen Kramer."

Charles should have added and the assault of Irina Curtius.

"You have the right to remain silent. Anything you say, may be used against you..." Charles continued.

I didn't think Alex would be able to say much of anything at this point. He certainly didn't even look like he was listening, only groaning in pain.

"You have the right to consult a lawyer..."

I kept staring at the back of Alex's head as he laid there. It all felt surreal except for my neck hurting. How did Charles know that he murdered Stephen?

Two police officers arrived. They said a concerned woman in the building had called 9-1-1. Leading Alex away, Charles called the precinct canceling the backup.

Charles put his arms around my shoulder.

"How did you know to check in here?" I said, half addressing Charles, half wondering aloud.

"The results of the water bottle contents came back. Antifreeze. We lifted Rankin's fingerprints off the bottle and ran them through a database. It turned out he has a history of being acquitted on charges including one of attempted murder in Chicago. An office-mate."

I gasped. "Most disturbing," I said, my voice breaking up. An uncontrollable shiver ran up and down my spine. "He was nasty from the first moment I met him."

"A real bad egg." He pulled me close and held me tightly in his arms. "Irina, you don't know how happy I was to be coming over this morning to bring you the news."

I looked up at him. "You know how happy *I* am. Thank you so much for showing up."

"If you hadn't been so persistent, we may never have looked into Stephen's death."

A few minutes later, Tricia came into the apartment from across the hall, with Alice in her footsteps. Both surveyed the scene with wide eyes. They looked from Charles to me. "Irina, what happened?" Tricia asked.

They had been home during all this? How could they not have heard me scream, multiple times, each time louder than before? I had often easily heard Tricia and Stephen arguing, even making out some of the words. Those two were nasty pieces of work. I knew they weren't the ones who called the police. I'm sure they now came over to deflect suspicion from themselves after seeing Alex being led into a police car. "Alex is what happened. As you well know."

Tricia shot a nervous glance towards Alice.

Charles told them it was best if they left this to the authorities at this time and ushered them out. He knew my suspicions.

After he closed the door, I asked, "What about them? There were two different poisons in Stephen's system. What are you going to do about them? Alex said, 'Alice was taking too long.' He had to finish the job."

Charles' lips were pressed together tightly. I could see a blood vessel throbbing in his forehead. "We'll deal with that. Don't worry about that now. I think I should take you to the hospital to be checked out." He put his arms around me.

"Not necessary. I'll be fine in a bit. Let's go in the kitchen. I could use a cup of tea to settle my nerves."

Charles looked at me with a worried expression. His forehead now wrinkled. "Are you sure?"

"Charles, I'm fine, really. I need some tea, though."

* * * *

That afternoon Jerome called to say he was stopping over on his way to work.

When I opened the door to him, I said, "If this is an attempt to try and get me back with Robert, you can turn right back around and leave. That's a closed book."

His voice cracked. "I came to apologize. I didn't get a chance to talk with you on Monday. I'm sorry I ever got you involved with Robert again. I didn't realize that he and Monica still had something going on. He told me it was over and I believed him. I trusted he was serious and I knew how good the two of you once were."

I rolled my eyes at him to make a point, but then I laughed. "Jerome, you're a dear friend. I know you meant well. But please, never feel the need to set me up again."

He then laughed as well.

"Besides, it happens I'm seeing someone, a friend from my ballet days. I don't know if anything romantic will evolve. We'll see."

Jerome looked excited. He was such a romantic. "That's excellent, Irina."

We sat down on the sofa while I told him about my harrowing morning and how I had put my ballet "finisher" move to good use. Despite the seriousness of the situation—not at all lost on Jerome—we both laughed.

"Ouch! You have strong legs. I think it's admirable you can laugh about such a scary episode."

I shrugged, then smiled. "What else can I do?"

He looked at his watch. "I want to put in a few hours at the lab this afternoon. Anthony and I are going out to dinner this evening. Perhaps we could double date some—"

"I don't want to talk about dating with you anytime soon."

Jerome laughed. "I'd better get going."

I gave him a peck on his cheek. "I'll see you tomorrow at the studio."

* * * *

That evening alone in my apartment with only Joni Mitchell to keep me company on my stereo, I poured myself a glass of wine in my dim, candlelit living room. I felt relieved. After forty years, I finally had closure regarding Robert and relief that Alex was in custody. At least one of Stephen's murderers would be brought to justice. I put my feet on the ottoman, took a deep breath, closed my eyes and listened to the beat of the music. So much had happened in the past few weeks. I felt serene. It was as if the evening, the music, the wine, the softness of the chair I was sitting on, all merged together creating pure tranquility, peace.

Not a thing could relinquish the calm in my spirit. I smiled.

Chapter Twenty-One

Wednesday, March 4

When I walked out into the hallway on my way to the ballet studio, I did a double-take seeing Celeste coming down the stairs, being taken away in handcuffs by two police officers. My mouth fell open. What was going on? Was she also somehow connected with Stephen's death? She looked at me and half-smiled as she passed by and was led out the door.

After Celeste and the police officers left the building, I went back into my apartment and called Charles.

"We were tipped off from a renter in one of the neighboring brownstones regarding the robberies. Celeste was recognized leaving an apartment that was robbed a few days ago. A warrant was issued and this morning her apartment searched. Many of the reported stolen goods in the rash of apartment break-ins were found."

I went over to the sofa and sat down, putting my bag on the coffee table. "That's so hard to believe of Celeste. She was always so friendly and seemed forthcoming." Then I thought back to when she was jiggling Tricia and Alice's door handle. My heart started to race. Margarite and I were lucky someone came through the front door that day resulting in Celeste walking away.

"It's a shame. I enjoyed talking to her at Stephen's funeral. She was quite the interesting woman."

I fiddled with the handle of my bag. "I still can't believe it of Celeste?"

"The call that was made to the police department yesterday, about your screaming, was traced back to her apartment."

"Oh, my, gosh! Celeste was my good Samaritan? And now this?"

"Yes. I drove by your apartment today. I saw a FOR SALE sign in your neighbors', Tricia and Alice's window. You'll definitely be getting new neighbors."

Charles had a strange tone when he mentioned the new neighbors.

"I had no idea a sign was up. It must have gone up early this morning. Tricia had mentioned previously about putting the apartment up for sale. I still can't believe they aren't being charged with attempted murder?"

"They were brought to police headquarters late last night. I'm surprised you didn't see the police arrive. I was expecting your call." He snickered.

I rolled my eyes. "I fell a sleep in the living room listening to music. When I woke up, I went to bed and was dead to the world. What happened?"

"Both were taken separately and each consistently maintained their and the other's innocence."

My posture stiffened. "Of course they would. They always seem to be in sync with each other in their cover-ups and lies. I told you Alex confessed that Alice was poisoning Stephen." I mentioned again about the flowers at the Korean market where they shopped.

"Even if they had been seen buying the flowers, it wouldn't prove they put them in Stephen's food."

"They're guilty. They're going to get away with it." I could feel my blood pressure go up.

"Unfortunately, there wasn't anything we could do at the time, if they maintained their stories, unless one came forward against the other. We let them go."

"Little to no chance of that happening. Their thick as...murderers. What do you mean at the time?"

Charles hesitated for several seconds, too long. I could hear him breathing so I knew we weren't disconnected. Something was up.

"Charles?"

"On the bright side, we never would have had Alex in custody, had you not retrieved the water bottle. Irina, you really should add detective to your list of many talents."

"Why, thank you." I wish I would have been able to pin something on the sisters. "Charles what aren't you telling me? I can tell by your tone of voice. You sound like the cat that ate the canary or whatever that saying is."

"There's an art opening this weekend. Would you be interested in going?"

"I'd love to. But Charles, don't change the subject. I know something is going on?"

"We have a squad car coming to pick the sisters up within the hour."

I leaned forward on the sofa. "What? What happened?"

"This morning when I was in the interrogation room, I mentioned something to Alex about the sisters."

My eyes went wide. "Did you tell him they tipped off the police?"

"Nothing that could be considered entrapment, but he asked exactly the same thing. I didn't want you living next to those two. When I didn't respond and just looked at him, he must have assumed they did."

"That was great thinking."

"He said he wasn't going down alone and he went ahead and dragged them down with him. He's testified that the sisters were trying to poison Stephen, at first with herbs to weaken his health and then the flowers were to finish the job. Alex said 'He just hurried the process along.'"

"Both of them?"

"That's what he said. He signed a written statement."

My head started to throb. How could Tricia have done this to Stephen? "Quite the conspiracy. Alex isn't going to get a lighter sentence because of this, is he? I hope this wasn't a plea deal."

"He isn't and it wasn't. He just didn't want to take the rap alone."

"I know why Alex wanted to kill Stephen, but did you ask him why Tricia and Alice wanted to kill him?" I bit at my bottom lip.

"Stephen had a two million dollar life insurance policy and they had found the divorce papers. We'll learn more when we bring them in today."

I shook my head. I bet Alice talked Tricia into this. Still, she didn't have to go along with it. "How vile. And to think that I considered Tricia my friend. She sure changed." I bet this started long before they discovered the divorce papers.

Charles ended the call with a warning, to stay away from Tricia and Alice this morning.

After we hung up, I tried to stifle any more thoughts of hate, betrayal, and death. I left once again for the studio. Passing our building, I looked up and saw the FOR SALE sign in the window of Tricia's apartment. Tricia was looking out, watching me as I walked by. I turned my head and focused straight ahead of me.

On the way, I thought about how each moment of life was precious and to make every second count. Michel would be a big part of that. I would use my time wisely. I had read something similar to this in a mindfulness article. I smiled. All of a sudden the world seemed brighter.

I found myself humming as I turned the corner and arrived at my studio. I glanced up at the Little Cygnet's Ballet

Academy sign on the awning and smiled again. My bliss. I took a deep breath still looking at the words, held it for a few seconds, then let it out.

"Miss Irina! Miss Irina!"

I turned and saw Ivy running towards me, her mother half a block behind.

I put my arm around her shoulder. "Ivy, how lovely to see you and your mother."

"I missed seeing you on Monday, Miss Irina," Ivy said. "I've been practicing my...."

We walked into the studio.

ABOUT THE AUTHOR

Susan Bernhardt has had a love affair with New York City from way back. She lives in northern Wisconsin with her husband and has two sons.

Susan is a member of Sisters in Crime, Inc. and the Wisconsin Writers Association. Her published works include: *The Ginseng Conspiracy*, *Murder Under the Tree*, *Murder by Fireworks*, *Paradise Can Be Murder*, "October 31st", "Midsummer", and "John and Madeline."

When not writing, Susan loves to travel, bicycle, kayak, and create culinary magic in her kitchen. She works in stained-glass, daydreams in her organic garden, stays up late reading mysteries, and eats lots of chocolate.

The Kay Driscoll Mysteries
by
Susan Bernhardt

The Ginseng Conspiracy
Murder comes to town and so does Kay Driscoll, whose tenacious nature tells her city officials are attempting a cover-up and she must expose the truth.

Murder Under the Tree
During the season of peace on earth, good will to men, Kay uncovers sinister plots of corruption at a retirement home, while investigating the suspicious death of a beloved caretaker.

Murder by Fireworks
An obnoxious member of Kay's book club is found dead on the beach. When Kay investigates, she discovers that the death, covered-up to look like suicide, was in fact murder.

Paradise Can Be Murder
Kay's cruise with family and friends soon leads to a murder investigation on the high seas, and the clock is ticking to find justice for the victim before their time in paradise ends.

Made in the USA
Columbia, SC
16 January 2019